W9-BMW-930

GORDON KORMAN

BUGS POTTER
LIVE AT NICKANINNY

For everyone who supported Bugs the first time out.

GORDON KORMAN
BUGS POTTER
LIVE AT NICKANINNY

Cover by Laurie McGaw

Scholastic-TAB Publications Ltd.
123 Newkirk Road, Richmond Hill, Ontario, Canada

Copyright © 1983 by Gordon Korman. All rights reserved.

Canadian Cataloguing in Publication Data

Korman, Gordon
  Bugs Potter live at Nickaninny

ISBN 0-590-71225-X

I. Title.

PS8571.075B83   jC813'.54   C83-098394-5
PZ7.K67Bu

No part of this publication may be reproduced, or stored in a retrieval system, or transmitted in any form or by any means, electronic, mechanical, photocopying, recording, or otherwise, without written permission of the publisher, Scholastic-TAB Publications Ltd., 123 Newkirk Road, Richmond Hill, Ontario, Canada L4C 3G5.

2nd printing 1983   **Printed in Canada**
                    Manufactured by Webcom Limited

Contents

Back to nature

Bugs Potter sat at his drum set between two blasting stereo speakers, arms and drumsticks flying as he played along with "Liberation Day" by Endomorph. His face was blissful. Only ten minutes earlier school had officially ended for the year and Bugs was celebrating with a rousing rendition of one of his favourite songs.

"David!"

The call from upstairs was drowned out by the roar of the music.

"*David!*"

The basement lights flashed on and off in signal. Bugs turned the volume dial from nine-and-a-half to eight.

"Yeah?"

"Would you turn that row off and come up here?" bellowed Frank Potter, Bugs' father.

"Pardon me?"

His father stomped down the stairs holding his ears, marched over to the stereo and switched it off. An oppressive quiet descended.

"You called me, Dad?"

"Yes, I called you. How many times do I have to tell you not to play that thing so loud? There are other people in this neighbourhood, you know. Mr. Lee has complained that he can't hear his lawn-mower."

Bugs shrugged. "Sorry." He reached for the *on* switch. "Is that all?"

Frank Potter sighed. "No, it's not all. Come on upstairs. I want to discuss our vacation plans with you."

"Oh, you don't need me for that," said Bugs, flipping a drumstick and catching it. He indicated a calendar tacked to the wall beside the stereo; elaborate notes were scribbled in almost every square. "I'm pretty well booked up until Labour Day."

His father looked at the calendar. Apparently David expected to spend his entire summer attending rock concerts and festivals across North America. "Come on. Upstairs."

Bugs followed his father up to the kitchen where two cups of tea sat on the table. Father and son seated themselves, and Mr. Potter spread out a large map. With a pencil he pointed to a spot far north in the province of Ontario.

"This is where we're going—Lake Naka-mee-chee."

Bugs sprayed tea all over the map. "*What?*" he choked.

"Lake Naka-mee-chee," his father repeated patiently. "This family is getting soft and citified. We need to get away from modern conveniences and the pressures of city life. We're going camping for two weeks in a wilderness paradise far from cars and lawnmowers and television."

Bugs' face had lost all its colour. "But Dad—" He pointed one drumstick at Winnipeg, where the Potters lived, and the other at the small blue dot at the top of the map. "It's so far! It'll be a really long drive."

"Oh, you can't drive to Lake Naka-mee-chee. You have to be flown in by float plane. It's completely isolated from the outside world." Mr. Potter paused briefly while Bugs moaned. "For years I've felt the urge to get back to nature. I haven't done anything like this since my old days as a Queen Scout. I know it may not be what you have planned, David, but it'll be good for you, good for all of us. I just can't explain it to you—the joy of it all, the smell of the air, chopping wood, cooking over a fire, hunting, fishing, bathing in an ice-cold lake!"

Bugs looked more ill than impressed. "Mom will never buy it," he said hopefully.

"Of course she will! In fact, she's looking forward to it."

"Oh."

"Cheer up, David," his father said kindly. "You'll enjoy it when you get there."

"But where are we going to live? Is there a hotel?"

"Of course not. We'll be in a tent."

"A tent? But where will we plug in the stereo?"

"We're not taking the stereo, David."

Bugs was aghast. "No stereo? I suppose the next thing you'll tell me is that I can't take my drums!"

"That's right. No drums," said Mr. Potter. "Everything has to go by plane so we're going with

3

a minimum of luggage. We're really going to rough it."

"But Dad, listen to reason! If we're going to be up there at Lake Nickaninny—"

"Naka-mee-chee."

"Yeah. If we're going to be there, how am I going to get down to New York for the big Black Hole concert? They don't tour very often, you know. I've just got to see their new drummer!"

"That's just the point, David," said his father firmly. "A hobby is a hobby, but rock music is your whole life, to the exclusion of everything else. There will be no rock music on this trip. None."

"Dad!" cried Bugs, horrified. "You mean I can't even bring along my portable tape deck?"

"That's right. No rock music at all. You'll have time to work on that make-up science assignment you're supposed to do this summer."

"How did you know about that?" asked Bugs in a small voice.

"Your teacher called today. Really, David— thirty-eight percent in science! For the son of a research chemist that's disgraceful. And it's more than a coincidence that you failed your physics test the very day after you were out until four a.m. seeing that rock group."

"Powdered Sugar," Bugs reminisced. "What a concert!"

"And what a mark. Not to mention chemistry— terrible. And biology—worse! You're lucky the science department is allowing you to do this assignment to pull your mark up to fifty!"

"But I can't do school in the summer!"

"Well, you certainly didn't do any in the fall, winter or spring. Now you have to do it in the summer. You can write a report on Naka-mee-chee wildlife."

Bugs moaned pitifully. "It's going to be terrible, Dad. Really, it is! We'll—we'll be all alone!"

"No, we won't. We'll have lots of company. The Veddas are coming along."

"Oh, no! Not the Veddas! Anybody but the Veddas!"

"Nonsense. We've been friends for years," said Mr. Potter. "And you'll have Elizabeth for company."

"Elizabeth Vedda hates me. And her little brother —that's not company."

Just then Bugs' mother came into the kitchen, hiding her amusement at the sight of her son's green face. "I see you've told him."

Bugs threw out his arms in despair. "But Mom— Dad—it's going to be *boring!*" With that he rushed downstairs, flipped over the Endomorph record and began drumming mournfully to the strains of "Sent Up the River." Somehow he was going to get out of this.

* * *

Elizabeth Vedda stared in disbelief at the large map. "You're kidding!"

"Aren't you pleased?" asked her father. "An interesting and unusual idea for a vacation, don't you think?"

"A crazy idea for a vacation!" cried Elizabeth. "Who came up with this horror?"

"Frank Potter and I," said John Vedda with pride. "We're going up there with his family."

"Never!" thundered Elizabeth. "I wouldn't go around the corner with Bugs Potter and his incessant drumming! I'm not going."

"Of course you are, dear. We're all going as a family."

"And Mother gave permission?" Elizabeth asked, incredulous. She could not picture her fastidious, stylish mother roughing it at Lake Naka-mee-chee.

"Well, I'll admit she took a little convincing at first. But when I promised to buy her a new wardrobe for the trip, she brightened up immediately. She and Peter are really looking forward to it now."

Elizabeth slumped in her chair. "I don't believe it. We don't know anything about camping. We'll die like dogs up there!"

"Don't worry, Princess," soothed Mr. Vedda. "Frank Potter was a Queen Scout, and your old father can do anything he can do."

"But Daddy, you're a civil servant. You don't know anything about survival. You had hysterics when the automatic garage-door opener broke down. The biggest thing you've survived is an eight-minute power failure!"

"Now, now, Elizabeth, that's unkind. We're going, and that's final. You'll love it. And it's a nice change from our usual cruise."

Elizabeth stared at the map. "Lake Naka-mee-chee!" Somehow she had to find a way to get out of this.

* * *

This was the worst thing that had ever happened to him, Bugs reflected glumly as he stared listlessly out the window of the float plane. Every turn of the propeller was carrying him farther away from everything he held dear—the Black Hole concert, the Turquoise Tuxedo TV special, the rock festival featuring Bay Leaf, The Antennae, Broadloom, Mushroom Soup and other immortal greats. And where would he be? Lake Nickaninny. It was too much!

Despite his grief during the preparation period, Bugs had managed to think rationally about the two weeks that lay ahead. He had invested some of his concert-ticket money in chocolate bars, a collection one hundred strong that would keep him supplied with real food for the whole trip. In addition, he had removed most of the carefully folded clothing his mother had packed for him and replaced it with his portable tape deck. He glanced uneasily at his father, sitting at the front of the cabin. Dad would thank him for this when he realized how boring it was up there. But just in case Dad didn't, he'd brought along headphones.

All his gear had caused a real space problem in his suitcase, and because he needed at least one change of clothing, he had cassette tapes, drumsticks and batteries for the tape deck stashed all over his body. At the airport he had had to walk with extreme care to avoid giving himself away by clanking.

Mr. Potter turned around in his seat. "So, David, you and Elizabeth haven't seen each other in a long time. I guess you must have a lot of catching up to do." He added meaningfully, "Right, David?"

7

"Hey, Elizabeth," Bugs began conversationally, "what do you think of the new Sump Pump album?"

She stared right through him. "I haven't heard it."

Good, thought Bugs, settling back into his seat. He had made conversation. That was over with. There was no talking to Elizabeth anyway—she wasn't interested in anything important. Besides, she was busy playing tic-tac-toe with her nine-year-old brother.

"Peter, you can't put an *X* there. My *O* is there already."

"No, it isn't!"

"Now, children," Regina Vedda's voice came from the depths of the current *Paris Fashion Guide,* "no fighting. This is the beginning of two wonderful weeks for all of us."

"That's the spirit, Cupcake," said her husband. "I'm glad to see you're not still upset about having to leave the Cuisinart at home."

"Well," said Mrs. Vedda, "as Frank says, 'When you're roughing it...'"

"I win!" cried Peter, drawing a line through two *X*'s and an *O.*

Mr. Potter turned to the pilot. "I guess you make quite a few flights up here."

The man laughed. "Brought a fisherman up once —think it was 1961. Never did find out what happened to him."

Elizabeth looked ill. "You mean he never came out again?"

Mr. Vedda laughed heartily. Heartiness, an essential attribute of the outdoorsman, was something he had been practising in front of the mirror for days. "He's just teasing you, Princess. Right, Frank?"

Mr. Potter laughed too. "Hang on, everybody," he said excitedly. "We're almost there."

* * *

Dr. Philbert Ramsay and Dr. Gerald Hyde, both Oxford-educated anthropologists, were sitting by their campfire deep in the Naka-mee-chee woods.

Hyde was stirring a large pot of soup. "I don't know," he said to his companion, who was studying a map. "We've been looking at various sites around here for the past three months and we haven't found a single artifact that proves the lost tribe ever existed."

"Still, some trace has to be here," said Ramsay without looking up from his map, "and you and I both know it."

"But what if there's some kind of flaw in our reasoning?"

"How could there possibly be? We've gone over it literally thousands of times. It represents years of painstaking research, of interpolating, extrapolating, interfacing and impacting. We've checked migration patterns of all the other local tribes, their trading habits and artifacts. The chance of there not having been another tribe here is one in a million. We'd be fools to stop looking now."

Hyde nodded. "I know, I know. I suppose I'm just a little tired today."

"Don't worry. If we look hard enough," Ramsay

said confidently, "we'll find traces of the lost Naka-mee-chee tribe. All we need is patience."

Hyde took the spoon out of the pot and put it to his lips. "Soup's ready."

"Good. We can't hunt after a Nobel Prize on empty stomachs."

Both men sat down and began to eat.

"Look, Ramsay—a plane! We haven't seen one since we got here."

"Confound it!" cried Ramsay. "It's going to land on the lake!"

"Do you suppose other people could be after our lost tribe?"

"They'd better not be," said Ramsay grimly, "because I don't intend to share any of the glory. I've spent years working on this."

"Don't you mean *we've* spent years working on this?"

"Of course, of course. A slip of the tongue."

No people?

From the air Lake Naka-mee-chee was a beautiful sight. The sun glistened on the calm water, a jewelled centrepiece in a scenic panorama. The lake was framed by dense greenery that stretched to the horizon in all directions.

Bugs watched as the lake began to grow and the features of the landscape became more distinct. When the pilot finally set the plane down on the bright water near one shore, Lake Naka-mee-chee stretched as far as the eye could see.

Mr. Potter directed the pilot towards an area of sandy beach by a tree-lined clearing. Mr. Vedda was the first to disembark, bounding energetically through the hatch, determined to breathe in the party's first lungful of rugged outdoor air. He landed in knee-deep water and sank up to his ankles in soft sand.

Mr. Potter donned hip-waders and hopped out of the plane. "Well, John," he grinned, "now that you've got wet feet anyway, you may as well help me carry the gang and the equipment to shore."

Mr. Vedda glared at the pilot. "You might have warned me that you were going to land in the middle of the lake."

The man shrugged. "A lot of people know that float planes land on water, mister." He put on hip-waders himself. "I'll give you a hand with the gear."

In ten minutes, equipment and campers were safely on shore. Mr. Potter sighed contentedly. "Well, that's everything."

The pilot grinned at him strangely. "Okay. Have a nice—uh—vacation. See you in two weeks."

"Aren't you going to come back in a couple of days and check on us?" Bugs broke in. "You know—see how we're doing, maybe fly us home if we don't like it here?"

"It's not part of the service, young fellow. You're on your own."

Bugs felt a large lump work its way into his throat as he watched the plane move out to the middle of the lake and take off in a spray of white water. There went his last link to the Black Hole concert and the new Endomorph album. What could have been his best summer ever was biting the dust.

Mr. Potter glanced around the beach and inhaled deeply. "Just as I hoped—total solitude!"

Mrs. Vedda looked around in alarm. "Why, Frank, you're right! Goodness! Where *is* everybody?"

"We're all here, Cupcake," said her husband, struggling out of his wet hiking boots.

"No, I mean all the other campers. Where are they?"

"We struck it lucky," crowed Mr. Potter. "We've got the place all to ourselves."

"How awful!"

Amen, thought Elizabeth, looking around the clearing.

"But that's the whole point of roughing it," said Mr. Vedda, assuming his rugged expression. "To be alone with nature."

"Right," said Mr. Potter. "And the first thing to do is see about shelter. Let's break out the tents."

The Potters had their tent up in no time at all. Bugs' father was beginning to feel that old camping know-how that had been locked up inside him for so many years. It was great to be back in the woods again. He and Bugs carried the luggage and bedrolls inside.

"Frank," called Mary Potter, "maybe you'd better come out here."

Mr. Potter emerged to see a large muddle of heaving, sputtering, swearing canvas a few paces away.

"This lousy tent . . . it's defective! I've been given damaged goods! What use is a tent that won't stand up?"

"Let me give you a hand with that," offered Mr. Potter, grinning broadly.

"It's no use!" came John Vedda's muffled voice from somewhere inside the mess. "It's defective!"

Mr. Potter grasped one of the tent poles and set it upright.

"Just sit tight a minute, John." He beckoned to Bugs and the two of them set up the Veddas' tent.

Mr. Vedda emerged through the main flap. "Good work, Frank. You corrected the defect, I see."

"Oh, it wasn't defective, Mr. Vedda," Bugs explained. "You just forgot the poles."

"Ah, yes, the poles. You'd think they'd have the sense to put them in a more prominent place in the package, wouldn't you?" He examined the tent. "But an excellent finished product. Right, Regina?"

She was staring off into space.

"Regina?" He nudged her arm.

"No people," she said mournfully. "We're all alone."

* * *

Bugs dragged a plastic spoon across his tin plate and shoved some baked beans into his mouth. He chewed miserably.

"This will be our most luxurious meal," Mr. Potter was saying. "From now on, we earn what we eat."

"Right," Mr. Vedda agreed heartily.

"What if we don't earn anything?" asked Elizabeth, helping herself to a slice of whole-wheat bread.

Mr. Potter laughed. "I guess we go hungry."

Bugs thought happily of his suitcase full of chocolate bars.

"This food stinks!" announced Peter in his usual whining tone. "Ma, you didn't tell me we were going to be having stinky food!"

"I'm sorry, dear, but there isn't any good food here. Blame it on your father, not me. There isn't anything up here. Just us. Right, John?"

"Just us," her husband confirmed cheerfully.

"Have some more beans, Regina," offered Mary Potter.

"Good heavens, no. They're fattening."

"Not if they're your last meal for two weeks, Mother," muttered Elizabeth.

"Don't worry," grinned Mr. Potter, adding another piece of kindling to the fire. "Tomorrow we'll catch you a mess of fish to fry."

Elizabeth made a face. "Mess" was the operative word all right.

Frank Potter inhaled deeply. "Ah, the great outdoors! The crackle of the fire, the smell of the air! Look at the sun going down behind the trees. Isn't this glorious?"

"Indeed it is, Frank," said Mr. Vedda with enthusiasm.

"I don't care for your powder-room facilities," Mrs. Vedda interrupted.

"What powder-room facilities?" asked Mr. Potter. "Oh, you mean the Porta-Toilet. Well, I brought that along for you ladies. If we didn't have it we'd have to dig a latrine and—"

"Please, Frank, not at the—uh—campfire," begged his wife.

"Who knows some good campfire songs?" prompted Mr. Potter.

There was dead silence.

"How about our daughter singing for us?" suggested Mr. Vedda. "She's studying voice at the Royal Conservatory, you know. Go ahead, Elizabeth. Sing something."

"No."

"Oh, come on, Princess. We want to hear you sing. Isn't that right, folks?"

Bugs felt his father's elbow against his ribs. "Oh.

Yes," he choked.

Elizabeth pointed to her throat. "The beans are sitting just about there. Some other time maybe."

"Ma, when do we go home?" asked Peter.

She sighed. "In two weeks, darling."

* * *

As the rest of the company lay sleeping, Bugs sat propped up against a tree about a hundred metres from the campsite. His tape deck lay in his lap, the headphones pounding out the hard rock rhythms of *The Grape Album* by Fruit Juice. Bugs' eyes were closed and he was munching ravenously on a Fudge Coconut Ripple Bar while his hands drummed furiously on his knees.

He had gone almost twenty-four hours without any music, and his soul was refreshed as he listened to the pounding rhythms. He glanced distastefully at the stenographer's notebook and pencil that lay at his side. "For observations," his father had said. Observations for that stupid science project he had to do this summer. How on earth was he going to think up observations? Oh well, he mustn't cloud his thoughts with problems like that when there was important work to be done. He had to figure out a way to make some drums. If he could at least do that, the next two weeks would be almost bearable.

* * *

"Well, I guess there's no problem with those people," said Dr. Hyde. The two anthropologists had been down at the lakeshore to see who had arrived in the plane. They had spied on the small party and returned to their own camp well satisfied.

"They're just a couple of families on vacation," said Ramsay, "but they might accidentally stumble onto what we're looking for, and that would be very unfortunate indeed."

"Yes," Hyde agreed, "but there's nothing we can do about it."

"Of course there is. We'll simply make them hate it so much here that they'll radio for a plane and leave."

Hyde frowned. "I beg your pardon? Make them hate it here? What on earth do you mean?"

"On our way back from their campsite, I'm sure you noticed the portable toilet device they set up just inside the woods. Naturally they brought it because of the women and children. But if perchance it should disappear . . . "

"Ramsay, that's despicable—and unworthy of us! I refuse to help you steal a toilet. We are anthropologists, not toilet-snatchers."

"It's all in the name of science, Hyde. I'm as disturbed as you are by what must be done. But if removing their comfort station will drive those people away, then you must admit the end justifies the means."

"I admit nothing. We are here on a government grant through the Anthropological Museum of Ontario, which certainly doesn't give us the right to steal people's toilets. I refuse to be a party to it!"

"I never asked you to be. This is a one-man mission. All I ask is that you do not turn moral on me. And," Ramsay smiled broadly, "you must agree we've certainly been lacking such a facility over the past three months."

Primitive drums

"*Fire!*" screamed Mrs. Vedda, running in small circles around the breakfast campfire with smoke trailing from the hem of her silk hostess gown.

Mr. Vedda burst out of the tent. "Where's the fire? Where?" Heroically he pounced on the campfire and began stamping it out.

Bugs was just coming up from the lake with a large bucket of washing water. Elizabeth ran out of the tent, took in the scene and shouted to him, "Quick! Throw it on Mother!"

Bugs stared at her. "What?"

"*Throw it on my mother!*"

Bugs shrugged, then reared back and sloshed the entire bucket of water into Mrs. Vedda's face.

"No, you idiot!" cried Elizabeth. "Her skirt! Her skirt is on fire!"

Returning from his early morning jog on the beach, Frank Potter ambled over to Mrs. Vedda and kicked sand on the smouldering hem of her gown.

"Oh, thank you, Frank!" she quavered, sitting down on a rock to catch her breath.

"Fire!" shouted Mr. Vedda, dancing around, his

boot laces ablaze. Some outdoor common sense struck him, and he went tearing off across the beach to the water's edge, running into the lake until the water was as high as his knees.

Mrs. Potter was comforting Peter. "There, there, dear. Mommy and Daddy are fine now. It was nothing."

"Regina," said Frank Potter gently, "you don't wear long trailing skirts around a campfire. It's too dangerous. Why don't you dress more sensibly, like Mary or Elizabeth? You need scrubby old clothes."

Mrs. Vedda stiffened. "When I travel, I go first-class."

Mary Potter grinned at her husband and set about restoring the campfire. Mr. Vedda returned to the scene, his scorched boots making a squishing sound with each step.

"A lot of help *you* were!" said his wife coldly.

"Don't blame me, Cupcake," he replied. "Imagine those shoe manufacturers—selling people boots with flammable laces! What are you supposed to use to stamp out fires?"

"They're probably betting that the situation doesn't arise that often, Daddy," said Elizabeth.

"Well, that shows how much *they* know!" He stared at his wife. "Regina, you're all wet!"

She looked at him unkindly, then rushed into the tent where she could be heard rummaging around and muttering under her breath. A few minutes later she emerged wearing a silk blouse and a pair of skin-tight Bertrand St. René designer jeans.

"That's better, Regina," approved Frank Potter. "You don't want to wear good clothes to muck around a fire and clean fish and things like that."

She glared at him. "Clean fish? In my ninety-dollar Bertrand St. René's? Dont be absurd!" She went to help Mrs. Potter hang the large porridge pot over the now blazing campfire.

Bugs stared at the designer jeans and then at the pot hanging over the fire. Although he hated math, an instant equation popped into his mind:

*1 pair strong denim jeans + 1 porridge pot =
1 drum.*

* * *

Elizabeth Vedda and Mrs. Potter were lying on blankets on the beach, enjoying the early afternoon sun.

"I sure hope the boys catch some fish," said the older woman. "If they don't, we're going to be awfully hungry around here."

Elizabeth squinted, peering out at the small inflatable boat. "Well, I've been watching them for a while and it certainly doesn't look like they're reeling them in one after another."

Mrs. Potter laughed. "Give them time. They've only been out there twenty minutes or so."

An enormous royal velvet towel was flung out beside them and Mrs. Vedda, swathed in a gold lamé swimsuit, stretched out luxuriously on it. She produced a small crystal vial and began to spread scented oil on her body.

"I've decided to make the best of this horrid place," she announced, "by coming home with the most beautiful tan the entire Winnipeg Country Club has ever seen."

Mary Potter stretched. "The sun's really hot. Why don't we take a dip?"

"I'd love a swim," agreed Elizabeth, anxious for something to do. "Coming, Mother?"

"Goodness, no. I'm not finished tanning yet. This is the most expensive tanning lotion in the world— it's made from the oil of the emu liver, and emus are hard to find these days. Why, the only ones left live in Australia. This oil sells for a hundred and fifty dollars a bottle."

Elizabeth walked to the lake, stuck her foot in the water and sprang back with a cry of agony.

"You're right," agreed Mrs. Potter, making a similar experiment. "It's freezing. Okay, no dip."

"And no bath for two weeks!" added Elizabeth.

Mrs. Potter smiled. "Hey, look—there's some kind of commotion on the boat. Maybe they've caught something."

* * *

The four fishermen stared at the enormous clump of underwater weeds and reeds dangling from Mr. Vedda's hook.

Frank Potter laughed. "There's your whopper, John. Isn't he a beaut?"

Peter laughed too. "Boy, Dad, you sure are lousy at catching fish!"

Mr. Vedda's face flamed red. "Something must be wrong. Maybe the lure."

"Calm down, John. It could happen to anybody. Look on the bright side—you're the first one of us to catch anything at all. Let's just keep at it."

The four settled back down, dipped their rods in

the water and kept on fishing.

Bugs was daydreaming. He was in the front row at the big Egg Yolk concert. The lights were out and the audience was at fever pitch. Suddenly the searchlights illuminated a gigantic egg on the stage. With a tremendous explosion, the egg cracked open along a jagged line, spilling out dense yellow mist and revealing the four members of the group poised at their instruments. Immediately they swung into their number-one hit, "Sunny Side Up," from the *Boiled to Perfection* album.

Bugs absentmindedly put down his fishing rod and began to drum enthusiastically on the side of the boat.

"Cut it out, David," said his father sharply.

"What?" Bugs snapped out of the dream but continued drumming.

"Stop that. You're scaring the fish away."

A long silvery body suddenly broke water and flung itself into the boat where it landed at Bugs' feet, flapping languidly.

"A rainbow trout!" exclaimed Mr. Potter. "It's huge! I've never seen a trout that big!"

"Hey!" cried Peter. "Something's got my line!" He yanked with all his strength and a small pickerel came sailing out of the water, slapped his father on the side of the head and fell into the boat beside Bugs' trout. "I got a fish!" the boy cheered.

"I've got a bite too!" Mr. Potter carefully reeled in a good-sized lake trout. "Come on, David, put your line in. There are a lot of fish out there."

Bugs had gone back to his daydream about Egg Yolk.

"I've got another one!" cried Peter.

"Me too!" grinned Mr. Potter.

"This stupid fishing rod!" said Mr. Vedda in disgust. "It's good for nothing!"

"Isn't this fun, Dad?" cried Peter joyously.

"Quiet, son," said Mr. Vedda painfully. "You're scaring the fish."

*   *   *

Bugs walked through the woods carrying the large porridge pot and in it Mrs. Vedda's Bertrand St. René designer jeans. He had picked a good time to leave the campsite—his family and the Veddas were trying to decide who would clean the day's catch for supper. Determined to narrow the field by one, he had pinched pot and jeans and slipped into the woods unnoticed. He hoped Mrs. Vedda wouldn't miss her jeans: she seemed to have two dozen pairs with her and he was sure she wouldn't mind contributing one of them to a good cause for a few days.

He walked along for a while, mentally drumming to some songs from *Dorchester Melon's Greatest Hits*. Suddenly he stopped in his tracks, an annoyed frown on his face. Something was throwing him mentally off beat, and he had never been off beat in his entire life. He shut the music out of his mind and listened carefully. Something out there was drumming, and whatever it was had absolutely no rhythm at all. He moved forward slowly through the thickening underbrush.

There, halfway up a tree in the dense foliage of the thicket, was a small woodpecker pecking away at the bark. At the foot of the tree was the mouth of a cave.

"Perfect!" Bugs exclaimed aloud. This was the

ideal place to keep his tape deck, tapes and food supplies, and most important, to play the drums. He crouched down, entered the cave and looked around. Not bad—a little dusty, and the cobwebs would have to be cleaned out, but it was sheltered and dry.

He put down the pot and jeans, reached outside, broke off a branch and began to brush at the floor and walls of his cave. It was beginning to look like home already. Forget roughing it! He was going to spend all his time in his cave.

Bugs pulled Mrs. Vedda's jeans over the top of the porridge pot and found that the seat fit tightly across the opening. He left the cave and returned a few minutes later with a length of strong vine which he tied around the top of the pot, pulling the material as taut as possible. With another piece of vine, he hung the pot lid by its handle from a stalactite in the low ceiling. The lid hung at just the right height.

Now Bugs Potter had a drum and a cymbal. What more could a man ask for?

Gleefully he produced his drumsticks and began beating enthusiastically on the seat of Mrs. Vedda's jeans. The sound was a low-pitched thumping. He struck the pot lid and got something more like a metallic *clunk* than a cymbal crash. Well, he reflected, not exactly a drum fit for Endomorph or Migraine but, as his father would say, "When you're roughing it ... "

* * *

Dr. Ramsay dropped the reference book he had been reading and stood up like a shot. "Hyde! Listen!"

"What is it?" snapped Dr. Hyde. He was staring at the filched Porta-Toilet, his face registering a combination of guilt and dismay.

"Drums!" said Ramsay, quivering with excitement. "Primitive drums!"

Drums? wondered Hyde. Could Ramsay be getting a little tent-happy? But wait—"I hear them too!"

Both men stood still as statues, listening to the faint but distinct drumming sounds.

"It certainly doesn't follow any native drum pattern I've studied," said Hyde, perplexed. "As a matter of fact, it isn't even close to a known pattern. What could it be?"

As he listened, Ramsay's face slowly but surely broke into a broad smile. "The Naka-mee-chee tribe!"

"But that's impossible!" protested Hyde. "Our lost tribe couldn't possibly still be around today!"

"Yes, but there could very well be a small handful of Naka-mee-chee Indians who have survived in this remote place, hidden away, totally oblivious of the development of civilization outside. Do you realize what this could mean?"

"You mean to science?" Hyde was overwhelmed.

"No! To us! Think of it—a Nobel Prize, guest lectures, papers in all the scientific journals, maybe a book! Everlasting fame in the scientific community! We'll be rich!"

"We have to find the source of that drumming," said Hyde, who was of a practical turn of mind. "I wonder how it is that we've been here for three months and haven't heard anything before today."

"I'm sure there's a rational explanation. At any rate, you can't deny the existence of that drumming."

"We have to find the source immediately!" repeated Hyde decisively.

"Sometimes your simplicity alarms me," snapped Ramsay. "We must conduct the search in total secrecy. We'll wait a day or so until those campers are gone. And we need supplies. When we find our lost tribe we have to collect proper evidence of our discovery."

"Let's find them now!" urged Hyde excitedly.

Just then the distant drumming stopped abruptly. Hyde's face fell.

"Don't worry, Hyde. Ritual drumming never takes place in spurts that short. They're out there and they'll drum for a long time. We'll find them. Right now we'd better make a list of equipment to requisition. Now let's see, what will we need?"

* * *

"David Potter, where have you been?" Bugs' father was furious. "We're waiting for you to have dinner. And it's just like you to disappear when there's work to be done. Elizabeth had to clean all the fish by herself."

Bugs did nothing to hide his pleasure. "Sorry, Dad. I was off making observations."

"Where's your notebook?"

"I forgot to take it with me. But I have a very good memory."

"And Mr. Potter caught this one, this one and

this one," Peter was saying, pointing at the pan of fried fish. "And David caught the big one, and those four are mine."

"Oh, and how many did you catch, John?" Mrs. Vedda asked her husband.

"My equipment was defective," he replied, tight-lipped. "I'm very angry."

"We've been suffering a lot from defective equipment," Elizabeth observed. "I wonder why."

"It's luck," sulked her father, "and mine's all bad."

Mr. Potter began distributing portions of fish on tin plates. "Okay, everybody, dig in."

Mrs. Potter sampled the dinner. "It's really very good."

Mr. Vedda attacked his piece. "Yes, Mary. Fantastic. Catching your own dinner makes it taste better."

"How would you know, Dad?" piped Peter.

"Regina, *your* son is developing a big mouth."

Mrs. Vedda took a small bite and grudgingly admitted that the fish was delicious, although it would have been better with a dash of the secret sauce they served at that downtown restaurant where she knew the *maitre d'* personally.

Bugs took a bite of his dinner. What was so great about this? It tasted like fish. It had a *fishy* flavour.

Peter found the fish acceptable, and that left Elizabeth.

"Come on, Princess, try it," prompted her father.

Looking faintly ill, Elizabeth shook her head. "I know these fish better than their doctor," she said sadly. "Please pass the bread."

"You can't eat just bread for two weeks," said Mr. Potter.

"We'll see."

"Your turn to do the dishes tonight, David," said Mrs. Potter as she finished her meal.

Bugs looked up. "Oh. Okay." He had his eye on a small saucepan. With the deerskin vest Mrs. Vedda was wearing it would make a perfect snare drum.

His mother eyed him oddly. "You mean you're not going to try to get out of it?"

Bugs shrugged. "I've got to do my share."

"That's right," approved his father. "And be careful. We already seem to have lost our porridge pot somewhere."

While the others tried to remember exactly when they had last seen the pot, Elizabeth excused herself and started down the path towards the Porta-Toilet. She returned almost immediately.

"Uh—I don't want to spoil everybody's wonderful day, but I have to report that our restroom is gone."

"You're kidding!" Bugs exclaimed.

Elizabeth shook her head. "I'd never kid about something like that."

"That's impossible," said Mr. Potter. "You must have gone in the wrong direction."

"It's gone," Elizabeth repeated. "You can see for yourselves."

The whole party rushed into the woods. Mr. Vedda was first on the site. "She's right," he corroborated. "It *is* gone."

"That's just great!" exclaimed Mr. Potter in disgust.

"Frank, where can it be?" asked his wife with some alarm.

"Well, I certainly don't see what all the fuss is about," Mrs. Vedda announced. "Good riddance to it, I say. It was the most disgusting, unsanitary, primitive—"

"Yes, Mother," said Elizabeth, "but just think about what we're left with."

"It must have been knocked away a short distance by some animal," Mr. Potter decided. "Fan out and look around. It can't have gone far."

"My children and I do not fan out near large animals," said Mrs. Vedda primly. "Elizabeth, Peter —back to the beach at once. Coming, Mary?"

"Oh, come on, John," said Frank Potter. "We'll find it. David will help us."

Naturally the party did not turn up the Porta-Toilet. However, Mr. Potter and Bugs did manage to turn up Mr. Vedda after a forty-five-minute search that took them past sundown.

* * *

By moonlight a shadowy figure crept away from the sleeping campsite. It was one a.m. and Bugs Potter was setting up housekeeping. He carted his tape deck, tapes, drumsticks, batteries and chocolate bars —along with the saucepan and Mrs. Vedda's vest— through the woods to his cave, where he arranged everything neatly and efficiently. He paused long enough to devour a Bubble-Milk bar, then fashioned the new drum and sat down to test it.

Loading his tape deck with the new Volcanohead

cassette he donned the headphones and pounced on the drums, beating out the rhythms of the first song, "Lava Breath." The new drum made a remarkably good sound and was a welcome addition to Bugs' set.

* * *

"There they are again!" exclaimed Dr. Ramsay. "The drums!"

Looking at his watch, Hyde grabbed pen and notebook. "One-thirty a.m. this time. Hmmm. Five p.m. and now one-thirty. I've never heard of this before. The Naka-mee-chee tribe must be unlike any other we've ever encountered!"

Soaring Eagle, Son of Chief

The next morning saw a moral controversy at the Potter-Vedda campsite. All the campers were gathered around a small box trap Mr. Potter had set the night before. Inside cowered a large brown rabbit.

"Frank Potter, if you touch one hair on the head of that sweet little bunny I'll never speak to you again!" threatened Mrs. Vedda.

"But Regina," reasoned Mr. Potter, "we're roughing it, and this is meat. Wouldn't a rabbit stew go pretty good tonight?"

"No! Now let him go. John, make him let that poor creature go!"

"But Cupcake—"

"How would you like it if people twenty times your size trapped you in a box like that so they could make a stew out of you?"

"We have to eat, Regina," said Mr. Potter.

"Not at the expense of a little animal!" she insisted.

"Mother," Elizabeth put in drily, "you have three fur coats."

"That's different," said Mrs. Vedda smugly. "A coat's a necessity."

"You know, Dad," said Bugs, feeling rather queasy, "on Endomorph's *Ecological Retribution* album there's a song called 'The Last Rabbit Died.' If you heard that song you wouldn't feel so good about killing this rabbit."

Mr. Potter exploded. "Don't give me that rubbish about Endomorph! They're living high on the hog on plastic food, but we need this rabbit because we need meat. You weren't so squeamish about killing all those fish."

"Well, *fish!*" said Mrs. Vedda. "They aren't anything."

"Well, actually—"

"David," warned Mrs. Potter, "I don't think your father wants to hear what Endomorph has to say about fish."

Peter Vedda lifted up the box and the rabbit scurried off into the woods. "Oops," said the boy as an afterthought.

"Peter!" thundered Mr. Vedda. "You did that on purpose!"

"He looked at me, Dad," Peter whined. "I could never eat anything that looked at me."

"Well, that's just great!" said Mr. Potter in disgust. "Now would somebody please tell me what we're going to have for supper tonight? Our stew is gone and we're out one carrot."

"Don't get so upset about it, Frank," soothed his wife. "We could never eat rabbit anyway. We'll think of something for supper."

"Breakfast is ready," announced Elizabeth. "The eggs got hard-boiled during the ruckus—I hope nobody minds. And in case anybody's interested, we seem to have lost another pot."

"Another pot!" exclaimed Mr. Potter. "David, you did the dishes last night. Where did it go?"

"I washed everything you gave me," said Bugs honestly. "Maybe we just miscounted."

"We definitely lost the deepest saucepan," said Elizabeth.

"David, after breakfast you go up there and look for that pot."

"Sure, Dad," said Bugs. He was feeling the call of his drums.

* * *

Because his father was watching him, Bugs started down the beach towards the spot where he had washed the dishes. After going through the motions of searching for the lost pot, he headed into the woods, bound for his cave.

As he walked, drumming on his knee, a strange sound came to him—something like a moan. Following it, Bugs stepped over some low branches into a small clearing by a stream and gaped in surprise. There, lying unconscious beside an unlit campfire, was a long-haired, bare-chested Indian. He was young—perhaps a couple of years older than Bugs— and he wore fringed buckskin trousers and moccasins. Around him were signs that he had been camping there for a little while.

Quickly Bugs scooped some water out of the

stream with his hands and sprinkled it over the face of the Indian, who blinked and then slowly opened his eyes.

"Uh—how," said Bugs, raising his right hand Indian-fashion.

The Indian blinked again, focusing questioningly on the newcomer.

"How," said Bugs again. "Uh—me Bugs." He pointed to himself and repeated, "Bugs."

"Aw, cut it out, will you?" said the Indian, sitting up. "For crying out loud, this isn't the movies."

Bugs gaped. "Are you okay?"

"Yeah. Thanks for—uh—waking me up."

"Who are you?"

The Indian sighed. "My name is Soaring Eagle, Son of Chief, but you may as well call me Gus. Who am I trying to kid?"

"Are you a real Indian?"

Gus nodded. "One hundred percent."

"Do you live here?"

"Are you kidding? I'm a New Yorker. I live in Manhattan. The only reason I'm here is because my father, Chief Thundering Buffalo—"

"Your dad is a real Indian chief?"

"Well, yeah. But everyone he knows calls him Ted, and he runs the hot-dog concession at Yankee Stadium. He decided it was time for the heir-apparent to the chief to go back and find his heritage. So here I am. I've found my heritage. And no offense to my ancestors, but is it ever crummy!"

Bugs' eyes narrowed. "So you're the only other guy up here, right?"

Gus shrugged. "I guess so. I thought I was the

only guy up here. It's not much of a tourist attraction, you know."

"Then," Bugs concluded, "you must be the one who ripped off our toilet."

Gus looked blank. "Your toilet? You have a toilet?"

"We had one." Bugs scanned the small campsite. "What have you done with it?"

"Nothing. Honestly, I haven't got it. I was sent up here to live like my ancestors—they didn't have toilets."

"Oh," said Bugs. "Sorry. We've all been kind of touchy since it disappeared. Hey, I've got an idea. I've got a cave just a little ways from here. Why don't we go there now and toss back a couple of chocolate bars?"

Gus's eyes bulged. "You have chocolate bars? Real chocolate bars? I haven't had food in four days. I'm living off the land, just like my ancestors, except that I'm dying off the land. You know why you found me out cold? I caught a fish yesterday and I've been trying to clean it ever since. But every time I take a knife to it I pass out. What a heritage for a guy like me!"

Bugs gave Gus a mighty slap on the shoulder. "Hey, don't worry about that. We're going to be pals!"

Gus grinned weakly. "That's nice."

"We'll spend all our time together. We'll meet at the cave—hey, why don't you move into it? Great idea! Okay, let's move all your stuff there right now."

"Well, maybe I should stay here and live according to my heritage," said Gus uncertainly.

"You'll be crazy about my cave. It's amazing—for a cave. It's comfortable and dry."

"My father wants me to live the way my ancestors did."

"I'm sure that if your ancestors had known about my cave, they'd have moved right in."

Gus regarded Bugs oddly. There was nothing to say against such overpowering logic, and this guy was certainly anxious to be friendly. But it was a little disconcerting to be living off the land in perfect isolation one moment and sharing a chocolate bar the next.

The candy decided him. "I can be packed and out of here in five minutes."

*　*　*

"I understand exactly how you're feeling about your heritage," said Bugs, tapping absently with a drumstick on Mrs. Vedda's vest while Gus fell ravenously on the chocolate supply. "I've got the same problem. Take my dad, for instance. I love him and all that, but he's always getting into boring things like this camping stuff. That's why I'm here—it's his idea of a neat vacation, so we came with this creepy family, the Veddas. It's deadly."

Gus nodded enthusiastically. He wasn't sure what Bugs was talking about, but the introduction of a President Peanut Butter Fudge Nutty to his recently deprived system had put him in an agreeable mood.

"That's what makes our cave so great," Bugs went on. "My folks and the Veddas don't know about it. You've got to remember that I just moved in myself last night, so there hasn't been much time for it to develop—you know—the lived-in look. It'll seem better as soon as you unpack." He reached over and peered into the large knapsack that contained Gus's belongings. "Hey, far out!" Lovingly he pulled out a small handcrafted tom-tom. "A drum! Where'd you get it?"

"My father made it for me," said Gus. "It's supposed to add to the atmosphere of finding my heritage."

"Can I play it?" asked Bugs reverently. "Can I add it to my drum set?"

"Sure. Uh—drum set?"

Gus watched as Bugs placed the tom-tom beside the two pots he had already converted. The night before he had set the whole arrangement on a flat rock table beside another rock which served as a seat.

"Oh," said Gus. "*That* drum set. I was wondering what all that stuff was."

"It may look like junk," said Bugs, "but under the circumstances it's pretty good." He picked up a pair of drumsticks and tried a small roll on the tom-tom. "Hey, far out!"

"Well," said Gus, "thanks for the chocolate bars—"

"Hey, it must be amazing for you with your dad running the hot-dog stand at Yankee Stadium. You must get to see all the groups!"

"Well, yeah," said Gus. "The Yankees, the Red Sox, the Royals—"

"No, I mean the groups! *The* groups—Dorchester Melon, The Drips, Garbage, The Antennae, Endomorph!"

Gus looked blank. "Endomorph?"

Bugs was aghast. "Don't you listen to rock?"

"Well, I've heard a little . . . "

"That's terrible! Here, I'll play you some." Bugs popped a tape into the cassette player. "This is *Interior Contusion* by Endomorph, probably one of the best-selling albums in history. It's too bad we can't listen to it really loud, but if my dad finds the cave we're cooked. You should really pay attention to the drum sound, especially the bass." He hit the play button and the heavy metal music started.

Gus looked confused. What was so wonderful about this? It was—noisy.

Bugs could sit still no longer. "What a great song!" Picking up his sticks, he threw himself at the drums and began to play along.

* * *

Nineteen hundred kilometres due south of Lake Naka-mee-chee, two men sat over lunch in the staff cafeteria of the Anthropological Museum of Ontario in Toronto.

Dr. Vernon Sterling, chief anthropologist in charge of research, held a requisition slip out to his companion, Dr. Lesage, the youngest and newest member of his staff.

"What do you make of this, Jean-Guy?" asked Sterling. "It looks like Ramsay and Hyde are onto something, but they're being awfully stealthy about it."

Lesage examined the order. "It seems like an awful lot of equipment, Doctor," he agreed. "They wouldn't ask for all that photographic gear without having something to photograph. And all that sound equipment—what could they possibly need it for? And look—that must be the largest number of specimen containers ever. What are they up to at Lake Naka-mee-chee?"

"I don't trust Ramsay," said Sterling grimly, pouring out his tea. "He seems to be more concerned with fame and fortune for himself than with science. Besides, those two are working on a government grant through AMO. Whatever they discover belongs to the museum."

"Are you going to send them the equipment?" asked Lesage.

"Not right away," replied Sterling. "We'll let them sweat a little. When we have more information we'll decide whether or not they should get it." He paused to sip his tea. "That's why you're going to Lake Naka-mee-chee, to find out what they're up to."

Lesage choked. "But, sir—"

"No buts, Jean-Guy. This is extremely important to the museum."

"But I've never met Ramsay or Hyde, sir. I wouldn't even know what they look like."

"Here's a photo of both of them taken at this year's staff party. It's a little fuzzy and they look more—uh—relaxed than usual, but you should have no trouble recognizing them. And surely they'll be the only two people up there."

"But Dr. Sterling—"

"No buts! My secretary has booked a flight and requisitioned all the camping equipment you'll need. Think of it as a vacation, Jean-Guy."

Lesage nodded miserably. "My only question is, why me?"

"You've got the technical experience," said Sterling, "and you're clever and resourceful as well as being young and strong." And, he thought, because Lesage was the most junior person on staff, everyone else had had the seniority to say "Send Lesage." "I'm relying on you to bring back the answers. Now you'd better go home and pack."

* * *

Everyone at the Potter-Vedda campsite was enjoying their best dinner yet—roast pheasant. Mr. Potter had caught it in spite of John Vedda's "help."

"Can I have some more, Dad?" asked Bugs.

His father raised his eyebrows in surprise. "You had a whole drumstick. What did you do with it?"

Bugs smacked his lips. "Taking those scientific observations all day long sure gives a guy an appetite."

Mr. Potter smiled at his son and presented him with another generous helping of meat. When no one was looking Bugs wrapped it in a napkin and slipped it into his pocket.

"So," said Mr. Vedda, "what did you folks do this afternoon while Frank and I were out putting meat on the table?"

"Oh, we were just lying around," said Elizabeth, "the same as we did yesterday and the same as we'll probably be doing for the rest of our two weeks."

"Do any swimming?" asked Mr. Potter.

"Are you kidding, Frank?" laughed his wife. "I've had snow cones that were warmer than Lake Naka-mee-chee!"

"Well, we men will try it tomorrow. Right David?" said Mr. Potter, looking around. "David? Where has he gone now?"

*   *   *

Gus was grateful beyond words as he gnawed ravenously at the pheasant meat Bugs had given him. He topped off his dinner with a Cherry Cocoa Lump and sat down beside Bugs, truly full for the first time since he had come north in search of his heritage. The meal was so satisfying that he didn't mind when Bugs began to play along with "Hover Turtle" by Winged Tortoise.

*   *   *

Their ritual drumming is so primitive that it defies all description, wrote Dr. Hyde in his notebook. *In no other culture in Earth's history have such wild, erratic rhythmic patterns been developed so elaborately.*

"I really can't explain that drumming," he said, standing by the tent and trying to determine the direction the sound was coming from.

"Fascinating," said Ramsay. "We're on the verge of a discovery of gargantuan proportions. I wish those incompetents at the museum would hurry up and send the equipment we radioed for. Then we could get some of this down on tape."

"It seems to be coming from the northeast,"

mused Hyde. "The distance is difficult to estimate but it must be considerable. The sound is very faint, in spite of the fact that I'm sure there must be several drummers."

"That would explain the fullness of the sound."

"I wish I could be more definite about the direction. It seems to echo off every tree."

"Mmm-hmm," said Ramsay, glancing at his colleague's notebook. He should be making notes too, he decided. They would be very important when he wrote his memoirs.

Our new neighbour

Frank Potter stepped out of the tent into the cool early morning sunrise and took a deep exhilarating breath.

"Blast!" he exclaimed aloud, peering down the beach at a small tent which had sprouted, seemingly overnight, about seventy-five metres away. Trust some intruder to spoil their solitude by pitching camp so close by! He stepped over to the Veddas' tent and tapped a fingernail against the plastic window.

"Are you up, John?"

John Vedda crawled sleepily out of the tent, holding his blanket around him.

"Good morning, Frank. What's the matter?"

"Look at that!" Mr. Potter pointed indignantly.

Mr. Vedda squinted. "It's a tent," he concluded finally.

"I know that, but don't you realize what this means? We came up here for solitude and now somebody's moved in to spoil it."

"Well, of all the nerve!" John Vedda's indignation was aroused.

"Yes, well, there's nothing we can do about it. He's got as much right to be here as we do. I'm just annoyed because he camped so close."

"There must be some recourse," Mr. Vedda insisted. "Would this qualify as crowding?"

Mr. Potter laughed. "Forget it, John. I only woke you up so I could complain to someone. Let's build up the fire for breakfast."

* * *

Dr. Jean-Guy Lesage sat with his binoculars trained through the plastic window of his tent on Mr. Potter and Mr. Vedda. That would be them, he decided —Ramsay and Hyde. Even though he had accidentally machine-washed the photograph of them along with his shorts, he needed no more positive identification. It had to be them. They were the only people in sight. And they certainly *were* spending too much AMO money. A big, comfortable family-size tent for each man—it was almost criminal!

Then Lesage saw someone else—a tall, fair woman who seemed to be handling pots and pans. Had they actually brought a housemaid? Now one of the men was on his knees lighting the campfire. He seemed to be having trouble getting it going, discarding matches one after another. And there was another lady, but this one was no maid—she was dressed in a negligée that would have done credit to a queen's boudoir. A teenaged boy stepped out of one of the tents and a little boy out of the other. He rushed up to the unlit campfire and started pointing and laughing at the hapless man who was trying to light it. The man rose, threw down the matches and began stomping on them. Raised voices wafted on the wind towards Lesage's camp.

He dropped his binoculars into his lap. This was shocking! Ramsay and Hyde were using AMO grant money to take their families on a vacation! No wonder they hadn't reported back to the museum. It was despicable. Any casual observer would figure that they were simply two families on a camping trip, but he knew better. It didn't take a PhD to figure out that no one in his right mind would take his family out to this wilderness by choice. Dr. Sterling had been right. They were definitely up to something.

Another person emerged from one of the tents and Lesage quickly raised his binoculars again. His breath caught in his throat. Even from a distance he could tell that this was the most beautiful girl he had ever seen. She was tall and willowy, with long black hair, and even the rough camping clothes could not disguise her innocent grace. He watched, transfixed, as she went to calm the irate man who was now kicking wood all over the campsite.

He dropped his binoculars again. This was a terrible dilemma. He had caught Ramsay and Hyde wasting AMO money, but how could he blow the whistle on them without hurting the most beautiful, innocent girl he had ever seen?

* * *

When Bugs arrived at the cave he found Gus industriously chipping one stone against another.

"Hi. I brought you some breakfast." He handed

his friend a piece of fish and two slices of bread. "What are you doing?"

"Making arrows," mumbled Gus as he fell ravenously on the food. "I'm looking for my heritage, remember? When I get home I've got to be able to convince my dad that I found it."

Bugs held up a finished arrow, which consisted of stone arrowhead, wooden shaft and feathered end. "Hey, that's pretty neat. Uh—couldn't you find any straight branches?"

"That bad, huh?"

"Not really. It's a start anyway. Where'd you get the feathers? Did you catch a bird?"

"Are you kidding?" said Gus, resuming his stone work. "Me catch a bird? I found them lying around. That's why they're not straight like they should be. You've got to take what you can get. *Rats!*" he added as the stones in his hands both crumbled into pieces. He brushed his hands together in a gesture of dismissal, raising a small cloud of rock dust. "I'm a total loss at being an Indian and that upsets me. I'm depressed. Being a Naka-mee-chee down in New York is great—you live a normal city life and you've got a background you can be proud of. But up here the background becomes the foreground and it's no good anymore."

"Cheer up, Gus," said Bugs, loosely bouncing a drumstick on Mrs. Vedda's jeans. "I mean, you can't expect to be great at heritage right away. You just started. Even I wasn't that good at drumming when I first started—and look at me now! So what if your rocks fell apart? You've already got this arrow and it's—kind of okay. By the time you get back to New

York you'll be so good at being a Nickaninny that your dad'll freak out."

Gus smiled sadly. "Well, I appreciate the vote of confidence but—"

"I can help you," offered Bugs enthusiastically. "After all, we're pals. Between the two of us, we'll work at your heritage until we get it right. Feel better now?"

"Yes." Gus did, although he was sure it was not going to help him find his heritage.

"That's good. And now that I've helped you over the rough spots maybe you can do something for me. I'm supposed to be doing a science project this summer to pull my mark up to fifty percent. Whenever I come here I tell my dad that I'm making observations for it, but I think he's getting a little suspicious."

"What's the project on?"

Bugs shrugged expansively. "Your guess is as good as mine."

"That's a real bummer," said Gus sympathetically, "but I really can't help you. Last year my school guidance department took one look at my science marks and suggested I go into the arts."

"Well, I've just got to have some notes. My book is blank." Bugs looked around. "Dad says I should do it on something around Lake Nickaninny. What's here? Let's see." He peered out the small, well-covered mouth of the cave. "Trees, animals—no, too boring. Rocks—better, but I don't know anything about them." His eyes fell on Gus. "And Indians. Hey, I've got an idea!"

"What kind of idea?" asked Gus suspiciously.

"I could do my project on you. I'll just write a whole bunch of stuff on all the Nickaninny Indians from around here. That's scientific, isn't it?"

"Of course not," said Gus. "First of all, none of them live here. And there's nothing very Indian about them in New York. None of them are doing anything remotely Indian. Every so often Dad talks about a big family reunion up here and everybody tells him to forget it."

"That doesn't matter," said Bugs. "Indians are science and even unscientific Indians are better than no Indians at all."

Gus laughed. "I'll tell you anything you want to know."

* * *

"Confound it! I knew this was bound to happen sooner or later."

Ramsay and Hyde were sitting in a tree overlooking the beach.

"I know that man!" Ramsay went on. "His name is Lesage and he's one of Sterling's new flunkeys at AMO. I saw his picture in the last newsletter."

"Well," suggested Hyde, "perhaps we could use a little help searching for those Indians."

"I knew it was dangerous to radio in for equipment! Not only has it not arrived, but they've sent someone to spy on us!"

"Ramsay, we're on the same side as that young man. Why don't we fill him in on our activities here and pinpoint the source of that ritual drumming as quickly as possible?"

Ramsay looked at him pityingly. "What have I

been saying ever since we first heard that drumming? When we do this thing, we're going to do it right, with the proper sound and photographic equipment and proper specimens. We're not going to rush in and botch it up. And we're certainly not going to share our discovery with any partners."

"But what can we do now? We don't have the equipment and Sterling may never send it!"

Ramsay glanced again at the tent on the beach. "The first thing to do is get rid of that Lesage person. As long as he leaves here without having seen us, he'll have nothing to report. And how can Sterling give us trouble if he doesn't know what we're up to?"

Hyde puffed up like an enraged hen. "The last time you started talking like that we both became involved in a contemptible theft. And, I hasten to add, after we compromised ourselves both as scientists and as human beings, we are still left with the campers."

Ramsay was calm. "That simply means that the situation calls for the removal of something more essential than a mere toilet. We shall liberate Lesage's food supply."

* * *

"Well," said Mrs. Vedda, fresh from her afternoon nap, "what's for dinner?"

"Toasty Flakes," replied Elizabeth. "Today's fishing expedition didn't exactly break any records." She pointed at her father, Peter and Mr. Potter, who were all huddled in blankets around the fire. Without Bugs' help they had caught nothing, and in

Mr. Vedda's ensuing temper tantrum their boat had capsized. It was the last time any of them intended to try swimming in the lake.

"Hi, everybody," said Bugs, jogging up to the campsite. "What's new?"

The three fishermen moaned aloud.

"Our fathers went out to battle the elements," said Elizabeth, "and the elements won."

"Where have you been?" asked Mrs. Potter.

"Oh—around," said Bugs. "I've been working on my science project."

Mary Potter took her son aside. "David, when I did the laundry there wasn't one article of clothing belonging to you. Haven't you changed—" Luckily for Bugs she was diverted by her husband's voice.

"Aw, Regina, don't do that."

"Why not?" asked Mrs. Vedda. "What have you got against being neighbourly?"

"What's going on?" asked Mrs. Potter.

"I'm going to pay a social call on our new neighbour. I wish I had something nice to take him, like a cake or a bottle of wine. It would be so civilized."

"But Regina," said Mr. Potter, "it's supposed to be just us. And he probably came up here for solitude too."

"I am a social animal," said Mrs. Vedda haughtily. "When deprived of society, I wilt."

"I don't know about that man, Mother," said Elizabeth. "A couple of times today I could have sworn he was watching our campsite through his binoculars. I think he's a little weird."

"Of course he is, dear. He's at Lake Naka-mee-chee, isn't he? That doesn't deter me in the least—

I'm going over there. Anyone care to join me?"

There was dead silence.

"Well, I'm off then."

* * *

Jean-Guy Lesage watched nervously through his binoculars as the figure of the woman grew larger and larger. What could she possibly want? Had Ramsay and Hyde sent her to find out what he was up to?

There was a polite scratching at the canvas and he quickly hid his binoculars behind a large pyramid of canned goods.

Mrs. Vedda's elegant head peered through the tent flap. "Yoo-hoo. Hello there."

Lesage, who was pretending he was reading, dropped his book and jumped up clumsily. "Oh—uh —hello there." He paused and looked at her strangely.

"I'm Regina Vedda. I live in the green tent by the beach. How nice to have a new neighbour." She extended her hand in friendship.

Lesage shook it gingerly. "My name is Jean-Guy— I mean, uh—John Gee." He couldn't chance Ramsay and Hyde recognizing his name and connecting it with AMO.

"Pleased to meet you, Mr. Gee. What brings you to the neighbourhood?"

"Uh—camping," said Lesage. "I'm camping."

"Is there a Mrs. Gee?"

"Oh, no, I'm not married." What could Ramsay and Hyde possibly want to know that for?

"And what is your line of work, Mr. Gee?"

"Oh, I'm an anthro—I'm a welder."

"How charming. What sorts of things do you weld?"

"Uh—metal things. I specialize in metal."

"My husband is with the government and we have two children, Peter and Elizabeth."

So that was the name of the beauty—Elizabeth. His mind formed her name several times. And this was her mother. He mustn't throw her out, then, even though Ramsay and Hyde had sent her to spy on him under a phony name. Vedda! Couldn't they come up with anything better than that?

"Confidentially," said Mrs. Vedda, "I hate it up here. There's no one to have a conversation with, which is why I'm so pleased to make your acquaintance."

"Uh-huh."

"You really must come to dinner one night," she went on, "when we have food." She looked at the stack of canned goods behind him. "My, you're certainly well supplied. I guess you won't go hungry. Well, goodbye. Come over and say hello any time."

She marched off daintily, leaving Lesage in a state of mute hysteria. What an ordeal, he thought, slumping onto his sleeping bag. He was lucky he'd come through it. She was a shrewd interrogator, but he had held his own. Ramsay and Hyde might suspect he was after them but they had no proof.

He wondered if he should radio back to Dr. Sterling, then thought better of it. At least one innocent life—Elizabeth's—was involved in this mess. The final reckoning could wait at least a day until he'd had a chance to find out whether she knew what was going on. In the meantime he would lie low and avoid any radio contact with the museum. Determinedly he switched off his radio and turned his back on it.

* * *

"I've decided to do my project on Indians. I think Indians are scientific no matter what they're doing, simply because they're Indians and that's that. So if you don't consider some of my Indians very scientific, remember that they are. This is called 'anthropology,' and if that isn't scientific I don't know what is.

"In this project I will concentrate on a special group of Indians. These ones used to live at a place called Lake Nickaninny, where I am right now. Of course, they don't live here anymore. Who would? They have moved to New York and other places.

"How do I know all this? you may be asking yourself. I know because Gus told me. Gus is really Soaring Eagle and he is a Nickaninny Indian. He lives in New York with his mom and dad and sister but right now he's here with me."

Bugs looked up from his notepad. "That's all I've got so far. What do you think?"

Gus stared, eyes round with wonder. "Bugs, that's incredible! I've never heard anything like it before!"

"Oh, you like it, eh? Good. Anyway, that's enough school. What do you want to do?"

"How about some food gathering? My dad says our ancestors were food gatherers as well as hunters."

"That's a good idea," said Bugs. "We can get

some heritage done and then come back here and listen to some music. And if you don't mind, once we've gathered the food maybe I could have some of it for our camp. My folks and the Veddas didn't catch any fish today."

Each taking a hollow gourd from Gus's household possessions, the two climbed out of the cave. Bugs made a cursory survey of the woods around them. "So where's all the food?"

Gus laughed. "We have to find it. You know—nuts, berries, roots, mushrooms. Come on. I know where there are some wild berries."

Bugs followed Gus through dense foliage. "I can get into nuts and berries," he said, "but you can keep the roots and mushrooms."

Finally they came to a small clearing where they filled their gourds with berries, which were in abundance.

On the way back to the cave Bugs raved about the triumph the expedition represented. "We're a couple of food-gathering Nickaninnies, that's what we are! We picked these berries right up there with the best of them!"

At the mouth of the cave Gus swung a leg inside and froze. He looked from his own buckskin mocassins to his companion's canvas sneakers. "Bugs, look at this footprint. Were you wearing boots yesterday?"

"I don't have any boots up here—no room in my suitcase." Bugs looked down at the clear boot print in the soft earth in front of the cave.

"Well, somebody does," said Gus, "and whoever he is, he stood right here and had a good look inside."

Bugs turned pale. "Oh no! My dad! If he's found the cave, I'm dead! I'm not supposed to have my tape deck or drums, or even a cave. He'll kill me!"

"You'd really be in that much trouble?"

"More!" exclaimed Bugs. "Except—maybe it wasn't him. Maybe it was someone else—like Mr. Vedda. No, he'd just tell my dad. Who else is up here?"

Gus shrugged. "No one, I think."

"I can't ever go back to camp," mourned Bugs. Then he said more brightly, "Let's listen to some music. It'll cheer us up. I have some good Spoon Rest you've got to hear—it's their *Counting the Silverware* album. Come on."

* * *

Jean-Guy Lesage hauled his hissing inflatable boat out of the water onto the beach and began to drag it towards his tent. He had been on the lake all afternoon pretending to fish. In actual fact, he had kept the Potter-Vedda campsite under constant surveillance. He had been staring through binoculars and making notes on the various activities of the men he took to be Ramsay and Hyde, and on the comings and goings of the party during the afternoon. Everything had been all business until Elizabeth came out in a bikini to sun herself. At that point the notes ended abruptly and his memory was all grey. He hadn't put down the binoculars until a mishap with his pen had punctured the boat. Then he had paddled madly for shore to avoid sinking.

Exhausted and hungry, he entered his tent and lit the camp stove for supper. Stew, he thought. Yes, beef stew. He turned to his food supply and gasped in disbelief. Gone—a metre-high pyramid of canned goods, all gone! While he'd been out in the boat someone had stolen all his food!

Who could have done such a thing? There was only one answer: Ramsay and Hyde and their party were the only people in the area. And even though he had been watching their camp, they hadn't all been in view at the same time. They must have suspected he'd been watching them and stolen his food to chase him away!

What could he do about it? Not much, maybe, but he could go over there and pay back that awful woman's social call. And while he was there he would let them know—ever so subtly—that he knew they had stolen his food. Why, they were probably eating it right now!

* * *

"Ma," asked Peter, "if we're having our Toasty Flakes for supper, what are we going to have for breakfast?"

"Toasty Flakes again, dear. I guess it's Toasty Flakes from now on until Daddy takes us away from this terrible place."

"Please pass the stale bread," said Elizabeth politely.

"If it weren't for those berries David picked this would be inedible," announced Mrs. Vedda.

Bugs had brought some of the berries back to the campsite as a peace offering in the hope that if the boot prints in front of the cave belonged to his father the gift might soften the blow. At least it had made points in his favour.

"Don't worry, everybody," promised Mr. Vedda. "We'll be catching fish again and shooting game and we'll have lots of food."

"But *this* food stinks," announced Peter.

"I couldn't agree with you more," said his sister.

"It is pretty terrible, Frank," added Mrs. Potter.

"Okay, okay! If you think you can do better, *you* take over the food gathering."

"I believe I will," said Mrs. Potter. "Tomorrow the ladies will go fishing." She looked at the other two women. "How about it?"

"Sure," agreed Elizabeth listlessly.

"I do enjoy a boat ride," said Mrs. Vedda, "but I envision something a little larger and more luxurious ... "

"Yes," said Elizabeth, "but unfortunately the *Britannia* doesn't make any runs up Lake Naka-mee-chee." She glanced up. "Oh, no. Don't look now, but the creep is on his way over here."

"Oh, it's Mr. Gee!" announced Mrs. Vedda, rising graciously from the campfire. "Yoo-hoo! Mr. Gee!" She put her arm around the newcomer. "Everybody, this is John Gee, our new neighbour."

Half-hearted greetings were exchanged all around.

"So what can we do for you tonight, Mr. Gee?"

Lesage was transfixed, staring at Elizabeth. "What? Oh—uh—I've had a little problem. All my food has disappeared. I was wondering if you people —uh—know anything about that."

"Why, no," said Mr. Potter.

"Well," Lesage went on lamely, "seeing that you're the only other people up here, I thought maybe—"

Mr. Potter stood up. "Are you accusing us of stealing your food?"

"No, no, no! After all, it could have been any one of a hundred things, like, uh ... "

"A bear with a can opener?" Elizabeth suggested.

Lesage was speechless. She had spoken to him.

Mr. Vedda leapt to his feet. "I say, young man—" he began belligerently, but his wife grabbed him by the shoulders and forcibly sat him down again.

"Mr. Gee," said Elizabeth, "do you honestly think we'd be eating this slop if we'd stolen your food?"

"Oh, poor Mr. Gee!" said Mrs. Vedda.

"Please sit down, Mr. Gee," said Mrs. Potter sympathetically. "You're certainly welcome to what we have."

"But Mary," protested Mr. Vedda, "we don't have that much."

"Don't worry, John," said Mr. Potter sarcastically. "The women are going fishing tomorrow, remember? We're going to have more food than we know what to do with."

"You'll eat those words, Frank," his wife promised.

* * *

"This beef stew is delicious," said Dr. Ramsay. "Stealing that food was the best idea I've ever had."

"I absolutely refuse to eat it," said Hyde righteously. Arms folded, he stared his defiance at the tempting bowl of steaming meat and vegetables. "Stealing this food, even in the interests of science, was questionable. Eating it is downright unethical."

"Look at it this way, Hyde"—Ramsay did not

look up from his dinner—"Lesage won't be eating it, so why let it go to waste? There are children starving in Europe."

The aroma was weakening Hyde's resolve. "But Ramsay, this is very wrong."

"Well," said Ramsay, finishing, "if you don't want it ... " He reached out for Hyde's bowl.

Hyde snatched it away and held it to himself possessively. "See to your own plate!"

The Naka-mee-chee prowler

"Okay," said Bugs from behind his steno pad, "here's what we've got so far: *The first Indian I would like to talk about in this project is the Chief of all the Nickaninnies, Gus's Dad, Chief Thundering Buffalo.*"

"Bugs, if you want to get it right," Gus interrupted, "it's Naka-mee-chee."

"Well, we can iron out kinks like that once we've got everything down. Now listen: *Even though he really is Chief Thundering Buffalo, when the census taker comes he puts himself down as Theodore Nickaninny because everyone calls him Ted anyway, and in New York you have to have a name to put in the phone book. He has one of the best jobs in town. He owns the hot-dog concession at Yankee Stadium. Their slogan is 'While you watch the Yanks, Eat Ted's Franks.' The best part, of course, is that when there's a rock concert he gets to go for free. He drives a big Oldsmobile which Gus cracked up last year when he overslept and then tried to get to school on time for a big math exam. His dad almost killed him and he missed the exam anyway.*

"He is married to Gus's mom, who is named Tiny Doe, but everyone calls her Fanny. She is always worrying about her weight and has been on a diet for the last nine years. Nothing works, but everyone—"

"Bugs," began Gus, desperately trying—and failing—to string a bow, "I don't think this is what your science teacher has in mind."

"Of course not," said Bugs. "He doesn't expect to get anything. When he sees this he'll be thrilled."

"Yeah, but stuff about my mother's diet—"

"Don't worry," said Bugs. "It'll be great."

Gus laughed. "I want you to write to me next year and tell me what mark you got on this science project."

"Of course we'll write to each other. We're pals, aren't we?"

Gus stood up and stretched the bow he had just managed to string. *Snap!* "You see?" he said dejectedly. "Some Indian!"

"We need a break from heritage," Bugs decided. "We can do it later. Let's listen to some Chips." He started the tape. "This is their *Off the Old Block* album."

Gus looked thoughtful. "Bugs, are you absolutely sure it wasn't your father who left those footprints outside the cave?"

"Positive. If it'd been him I wouldn't be here now. I'd be dead."

"Yeah, but if it wasn't him, who was it? There's nobody else around."

Bugs punched absently at the hanging pot lid he

used for a cymbal. "You know, I've got a theory about that. At first I thought it was that Gee guy, but Mom and Peter both say he never left their sight yesterday. So that leaves the only guy up here except for you and me, my folks and the Veddas. Know who that is?"

"Who?"

"The guy who ripped off our toilet. He's on the loose around here somewhere. We were really lucky, Gus—we've got valuables in here and a guy who would steal a toilet would jump at a tape deck."

Gus frowned. "You're right, you know. Maybe you should tell your parents."

"Are you nuts? They don't know about the cave and we're going to keep it that way. But I can see we need some security around here."

"Security?"

"Sure. I'll bet the Nickaninny Indians were experts at camouflage. So we're going to combine security and heritage and cover up the mouth of our cave so well this guy will never find it again."

*　*　*

"Pray the fish are biting today," said Mrs. Potter, "or we'll never hear the end of it."

She and Elizabeth were sitting with their lines in the water. Mrs. Vedda sat at the opposite end of the boat spreading emu liver oil all over herself.

"The sun isn't really very strong up here in the north," she observed, examining herself. "My tan isn't progressing as well as I'd expected." She looked at Elizabeth, who was sleek and golden brown, and Mrs. Potter, who had a healthy reddish glow. "My goodness, you're both so dark!" She stared at the sun accusingly. "Why don't I tan like that? I use emu liver oil!"

"Maybe emu liver oil doesn't work, Mother."

"It *has* to work! It costs a fortune!"

Elizabeth squinted into the distance. "Wonderful," she said sarcastically. "The creep is out fishing."

"Oh, it's Mr. Gee!" said Mrs. Vedda with delight. "We must sail over and say hello."

"In case you hadn't noticed, Mother, we have no sail. All movement is achieved by rowing. You want to say hello to the creep, *you* row."

"Perhaps he'll come to say hello to us," said Mrs. Vedda vaguely.

"He doesn't have to," muttered Elizabeth. "He has those binoculars."

"I've got something!" announced Mrs. Potter triumphantly, reeling in a hefty brown trout. "There. At least we've caught one. I can't wait to see what Frank has to say."

"Congratulations, Mary," murmured Mrs. Vedda absently as she stretched out at the rear of the boat in an attempt to expose as much of herself as possible to the sun.

Elizabeth felt a tug on her line. "Here's another one. Oh, boy! Tonight we eat." She reeled in a large pickerel. "You should try this, Mother."

"Quiet, dear. I'm tanning."

A hundred metres away Lesage forcibly tore his eyes from his binoculars. Elizabeth was watching him and it was necessary to go through the motions of fishing. Drawing his rod back over his shoulder, he aimed and then cast the line forward. But instead of flying through the air and splashing into the water, his hook swayed back and forth in front of his eyes, a small piece of bright yellow rubber dangling from its tip, just the colour of—

"My boat!" he cried. Behind him he heard a familiar hissing noise and felt the boat under him becoming softer with every passing second. "Help!"

In the women's boat Mrs. Vedda sat bolt upright. "My goodness! Mr. Gee is in trouble!"

"What are you talking about, Mother?" asked Elizabeth peevishly.

"I don't hear anything," said Mrs. Potter.

"Don't just sit there! Do something!" Mrs. Vedda scrambled into the middle seat and began to row with long powerful strokes that propelled the boat swiftly through the water. The other two stared, amazed at her proficiency.

The cries for help were now audible to all, and they could see Lesage floundering in his almost-deflated boat.

"Don't worry, Mr. Gee! We'll save you!" screamed Mrs. Vedda.

By now Lesage was in the water, bobbing up and down in his life jacket, desperately trying to hold onto boat, binoculars and fishing line.

"Hang on, Mr. Gee!" cried Mrs. Potter. "Regina, row faster!"

Incredibly, Mrs. Vedda did.

Teeth chattering, Lesage watched as the women's boat approached at a rapid pace. Elizabeth was coming to save him. He could hear her strong young voice as the boat bore down on him.

"Mother! Stop the boat! You're going to kill him!"

"How do you stop this crazy thing? Hit the brakes!" screamed Mrs. Vedda.

Everything went momentarily dark as the rubber front of the boat bumped Lesage in the face, forcing him under. He bobbed up and was smacked over the head by a flailing oar as the boat lurched past him.

Mrs. Potter and Elizabeth managed to turn the boat around and pull up alongside him, hauling him, sputtering, on board.

"Oh, you poor darling!" fussed Mrs. Vedda. "What a horrifying experience! I declare, I feel quite faint!"

Elizabeth hauled in Lesage's binoculars, rod and what was left of his boat.

"Come on," said Mrs. Potter. "We've got enough fish for supper."

"Right," said Mrs. Vedda. "We've got to take poor dear Mr. Gee back to camp to get him dry and warm."

* * *

"Might I make an observation?" asked Dr. Hyde.

"Certainly," Ramsay replied without looking up from his book, which outlined the migratory habits of Algonquin Indians.

"The first thing I've noticed," began Hyde, "is that Lesage is still here. How do you explain away that little circumstance?"

Ramsay shrugged. "The plane was obviously delayed. Don't worry. It will appear, swoop down and take him away. Next question?"

"Our equipment has not yet arrived."

"That's simply due to the mule-headedness of Sterling and the others at AMO. They want in on our glory. But they'll send it eventually—there's no real hurry until the campers leave."

"Which brings us to my third point," said Hyde a bit nervously. "There hasn't been any drumming today. What if we lose our lost tribe? We haven't even found them yet."

Ramsay closed the book and stood up. "Hyde, without a doubt you are one of the worst worry-warts I have ever met. I can assure you that absolutely nothing is wrong with our situation. The Indians will still be here when we are ready for them. And we will still be rich, famous and acclaimed."

*   *   *

Bugs stretched the bow experimentally. "Perfect," he said, pleased with himself. "You see? This heritage stuff is no sweat at all."

"It took us all afternoon to get this far," Gus reminded him.

"Hey, don't worry about it. We'll get better with a little practice. Don't forget we also made a whole bunch of arrows—and two of them look like they might work. And we camouflaged the cave like experts. By the time we leave here we'll be the two best Nickaninny Indians in the world. Now let's test these arrows."

"You're not going to shoot at an animal, are you?" asked Gus faintly.

"Of course not. I'll shoot at that tree." Bugs fitted one of the good arrows into the bow, drew the string back and let fly. The arrow sailed through the air and twanged into a tall thin pine.

Gus was amazed. "Fantastic! You hit the tree dead on!"

"Well, not really," said Bugs. "I was aiming for the other tree. But I'm only two metres off," he added cheerfully. "You try."

Gus picked up the other good arrow. He fitted it to the bow, sighted along it and let go. He watched in amazement as the arrow sizzled past the tree where Bugs' arrow had stuck and disappeared into the forest. Both boys waited for the twanging sound that would mean it had struck wood.

There was an awkward silence. "Uh—great shot," said Bugs. "Too bad it didn't hit anything."

"I'm sorry," moaned Gus. "That's the way it always is for me. Now I've lost our best arrow."

"Hey, we'll find it," said Bugs. "Come on." He swung the bow over his shoulder and jogged into the trees, plucking the first arrow from the tall pine as he went by.

"How can we find it?" complained Gus, following.

"It shouldn't be too hard. Arrows fly in a straight line. If we go straight, we'll find it."

They walked for a little while, searching the underbrush, before Gus made the observation, "Well, we've gone straight and we haven't found it."

"Hmmm," said Bugs thoughtfully. "Maybe arrows *don't* fly in a straight line."

"Ours sure don't. And they sure don't fly this far. We've been walking for almost half an hour. I don't even think I could find the cave now."

"Don't worry," Bugs scoffed. "Two full-blooded Nickaninnies can't get lost in the Nickaninny woods —it's impossible! Now, we came here in a straight line—"

"How do you know it was a straight line? We walked around a lot of rocks and trees."

"Well, we'll use our native sense of direction. Let's go this way."

They walked for a little while longer, then Gus said hesitantly, "You know, Bugs, maybe it wasn't such a hot idea to camouflage the cave."

"Don't worry. It's around here somewhere. Hey, right over there! But there's a big hole in our camouflage!"

The two approached slowly. Bugs put a finger to his lips, motioning to Gus to stay outside. He fitted the remaining arrow to the bow and drew it back cautiously. Emitting a scream that he assumed to be the battle cry of the Naka-mee-chee, he burst in through the cave mouth, scattering leafy camouflage everywhere. Gus jumped in behind him. No one was there.

Bugs took stock of tape deck and chocolate bars. "Nothing's gone," he said in wonder.

Gus looked down at the tracks of boot prints on the cave floor. "Look, Bugs."

Bugs nodded. "It was him again—the guy who ripped off our toilet." He held out his hands in disbelief. "I can't figure out why he didn't steal the tape deck. And my tapes. They're priceless!"

Gus sat down on the floor. "You know, Bugs, if this person keeps coming in here maybe we'd better find another cave."

"No way. Where are you going to find another decent cave like this at a place like Lake Nickaninny?"

"Yes, but I'm the one who sleeps here, and I'm getting kind of nervous."

"Hmm. I see your point. You wouldn't want to get mugged at Lake Nickaninny." Bugs looked around the cave thoughtfully. "I've got an idea."

From Gus's belongings he removed two wooden stakes which he placed on either side of the mouth of the cave. Then he strung a length of vine across the opening and back into the cave, where he tied it to the *on* switch of the tape deck. "Watch this." He kicked at the vine, and the tug on the switch turned the tape deck on. "See, if someone comes in the music'll wake you up, and by the time he figures out what's going on you'll have our bow and arrow pointed right at him."

"All right," said Gus uncertainly. He didn't think much of the bow and arrow part, but at least the early warning would give him time to hide.

* * *

"Are you comfortable, Mr. Gee?" mimicked Frank Potter savagely as he and Mr. Vedda fried the fish for dinner. "Are you warm enough, Mr. Gee? Would you like another blanket, Mr. Gee? Have some more tea, Mr. Gee. *Drop dead, Mr. Gee!*" He shook his pan angrily over the fire.

"I know what you mean, Frank. Just because that idiot sank his own boat, Mary and Regina have adopted him."

"Oh, Mr. Gee," called Mrs. Vedda, "do put on my husband's slippers. Your feet look cold."

Bugs jogged into camp, his notebook under his arm. "Hi, everybody."

"David, where the devil have you been?" barked Mr. Potter.

"Oh—around. I've been working on my science project." Bugs patted his notebook. "I've got five pages done already."

"Really?" Mr. Potter grinned. "I knew this camping trip would be good for you. Come on. Get the dishes out. Supper's ready."

"And put out another plate," mumbled Elizabeth as she brushed past. "We're feeding the creep again tonight."

The two families sat down to dinner, Lesage between Mrs. Potter and Mrs. Vedda.

"Isn't the fish delicious?" exclaimed Mrs. Potter. "It's certainly a treat to eat something you yourself went out and caught."

The husbands were silent.

"Frank," said Mrs. Vedda, "you have a patch kit. After supper you can repair Mr. Gee's boat. And by the way, has anyone seen a pair of Bertrand St. René designer jeans? I distinctly remember packing four pairs, and now I can only find three."

Bugs chewed nonchalantly and thought of his first drum.

"Maybe at the last minute you decided to travel light, Mother, and only brought three," Elizabeth suggested.

"No, I had four. And I can't seem to find my deerskin vest either. Oh well, they'll probably turn up soon. Mr. Gee, why don't you try some berries with your fish?" She snatched his fork, speared a berry and a piece of fish and held them to his mouth.

"Regina," said John Vedda sternly, "I would like a word with you."

"Why don't you start the dishes, dear? While Frank repairs the boat the rest of us are going to play Old Maid with Mr. Gee. Elizabeth, get the cards..."

* * *

At the Anthropological Museum of Ontario in Toronto, the Department of Research was in an uproar.

"I know he's only been up there two days," Dr. Sterling was saying, "but when I call him I can't get through."

"He's probably busy following up on Ramsay and Hyde," said a senior advisor.

"Yes, but then our calls would just go unanswered. His radio isn't being ignored. It's dead. Something must have happened to the poor fellow."

"Or perhaps just to the radio," someone suggested.

"Would you like to take that chance?" asked Sterling. "What if the man is in trouble somewhere? No, I'm sending someone after him."

There was an uncomfortable stir.

"This time we're not taking chances with an inexperienced camper. I'm sending my nephew Benny."

There were relieved guffaws, instantly stifled. Sterling surveyed the group intently. "Well, come on. Out with it. What do you want to say? I can take it."

"Well," began a lab assistant carefully, "couldn't you find someone with a little more—uh—well, experience than Benny?"

There were titters from the others.

"I know, I know," sighed Sterling. "Benny's not the brightest boy in the world. But he's an excellent camper. I can't spare anyone else, and besides, I'm giving him the simplest instructions possible: find Lesage and report back."

Radio silence

"You see?" said Dr. Ramsay from his vantage point in the tree. "There's the plane for Lesage now."

"Why isn't he packed and waiting then?" asked Hyde, squinting in the early morning sun.

"He probably overslept. There's nothing to get up for when you have only water for breakfast. But the important thing is that he's leaving."

"Good! Now we can get out of this tree and start acting like scientists."

"Wait a minute!" said Ramsay. "What's this?"

Instead of picking up Lesage, the pilot was helping a young man unload equipment from the plane.

"Not another tourist!" moaned Hyde.

Ramsay slapped his hand over his eyes. "I can't believe it. No, it's not another tourist. Do you know who that is? Benny!"

"Sterling's nephew? The eighteen-year-old who sweeps up at the museum?"

"The very same," said Ramsay bleakly. "Sterling probably sent him to help out when Lesage radioed in that his food was gone. This is just dandy!"

"What are you going to do?"

"Well, obviously *we've* got to get rid of both of them. Let's see—Benny is supposed to have done a lot of camping, so he'll probably fish and hunt. The minute they leave their camp we'll move in and booby-trap something—maybe put a hole in their boat."

"Ramsay, this is getting out of hand. I'm a scientist, not a commando! And something could happen —what if somebody drowned?"

"Nonsense!" replied Ramsay. "Benny is an expert camper and they'll both be wearing life jackets. Nothing could possibly happen to them"—he chuckled—"except a jolly good dunking. And you do want to find the lost tribe, don't you?"

"Of course I do!" cried Hyde. "But we're not doing it. We haven't even looked for them yet."

"One thing at a time, Hyde, one thing at a time."

* * *

Benny Sterling quickly and expertly set up his tent, got all his gear in order and lit his breakfast campfire. He was frying eggs and brewing coffee when Lesage wandered out of his tent, yawning and stretching.

Benny broke into a wide grin. "Hey, it's you!" He ran over to Lesage, positively beaming. "Wow—I haven't even had breakfast yet and already I've found you!"

"Benny! What are you doing up here?"

"Uncle Vern sent me up to find you and report back. Is he ever going to be proud of me! I'm going to radio in right away."

Oh-oh, thought Lesage. If Benny reported back it would be the end of Ramsay and Hyde—and Elizabeth.

"No! I mean—wait a minute. First let me fill you in on what's going on around here." Benny was not known for his powers of perception, Lesage recalled. Maybe he could be convinced somehow that reporting in was the wrong thing to do. "I assume you know why I'm here."

"Why?" Benny looked blank.

Lesage stifled a grin. This was going to be even easier than he'd thought. "Can you spare some breakfast for a colleague? I'll tell you all about it."

Lesage devoured his breakfast with relish. A diet of fish, berries and Toasty Flakes was not suited to his appetite. "That was delicious," he said appreciatively, leaning back. "Thanks a lot. You're a great cook."

"Now do we radio Uncle Vern?" asked Benny anxiously.

"No. Listen carefully, Benny. We're here on an extremely important assignment for the museum."

"Yeah, I know. And if I don't call in Uncle Vern's going to be sore."

"Never mind that now. You see those two tents over there? The museum suspects the people in them."

"Of what?"

Lesage thought hard. "Of being up to something."

"Oh—yeah."

"What we have to do is infiltrate that campsite and find out what it is they're up to."

"So why can't I radio Uncle Vern?" asked Benny with a worried frown.

"Uh—er—radio silence. That's it. We have to maintain radio silence."

"Oh, I get it. Uh—why?"

"Because if they intercept our signal they'll know the museum sent us and they won't let us infiltrate. Do you understand?"

Benny thought it over for a long time. Finally he said, "Do you think we could infiltrate them real soon so I could call Uncle Vern before he gets sore?"

"As soon as we can," Lesage promised. "But we have to keep them under surveillance first."

"Oh—yeah."

* * *

The roar of electric guitars brought Gus to sudden consciousness. It took a second for his head to clear before he realized what the sound coming from the tape meant. An intruder was in the cave. Remembering his instructions, he reached blindly for the bow and arrow and began fumbling.

"Don't shoot!"

Framed in the entranceway stood Bugs, his hands over his head. "Sorry. I forgot about the burglar alarm. Hey, isn't this a great album? It's *Plastic Marmalade* by The Glob."

Gus waited for the beating of his heart to return to normal. "Bugs, don't ever do that again! I might have skewered you!"

Bugs laughed appreciatively. "I saw The Glob in concert once. Amazing! Anyway, I couldn't get you any breakfast. We're running out of Toasty Flakes,

so my dad's guarding them. You'd better eat this."
He tossed him a chocolate bar. "Maybe we'll find
some decent food when we're out doing heritage."

"I think I'd better start work on a war mask,"
decided Gus, rousing himself slowly. "My father
kept dropping hints that he'd like one to hang over
the fireplace in the rec room. Are you any good at
woodcarving?"

Bugs shrugged. "How hard can it be? We'll do the
carving outside so we can look for something to
eat."

They left the cave, taking care not to trip the
alarm again, and headed out into the woods. Gus
found a piece of wood he deemed acceptable and
Bugs discovered some blueberries.

"You know, we're getting good at heritage, but I
think food-gathering is our best subject," said Bugs,
pausing intermittently in his carving to pop a berry
into his mouth. ·

Gus was intent on his whittling. "Now remember,
it has to look fierce. It's supposed to strike terror
into the hearts of our enemies." He leaned back for
perspective. "Hmm. Looks like it should say *Have a
nice day* underneath."

"Not fierce enough, eh?" said Bugs. "We'll give
him mean eyebrows like this." He leaned forward to
make the adjustment. "There now, that's—"

"I think you've killed it. Now he looks like he's
winking."

"So it won't scare our enemies away." Bugs
shrugged. "At least it'll psych them out."

Gus had to laugh. "Well, if at first you don't
succeed—Hey, Bugs, what's the matter?"

Bugs was frowning, his hand cupped to his ear. "You know, I think I hear The Glob!"

"The alarm!" cried Gus, discarding the mask frizbee fashion. He and Bugs tore through the underbrush and arrived at the cave just in time to see a distant form melt into the woods.

"Let's get him!" shouted Bugs.

The two boys crashed into the brush after the fleeing figure, scratching, bumping, tripping and shouting encouragement at each other.

"He went left!"

"He went straight!"

"*Left!*"

"*Straight!*"

The two pursuers parted at ninety degrees. Gus thundered along, wondering why he wasn't running in the opposite direction, away from the intruder who was haunting their cave. Finally exhausted, he went to look for Bugs and found him standing stock-still in the woods.

"Well, we lost him," Gus puffed.

Bugs was staring intently at a large hollow stump sitting on a bed of pine needles.

"Look," he said with reverence. "You see that? That's my bass drum."

* * *

From their boat out in the middle of the lake Lesage and Benny trained their binoculars on the Potter-Vedda campsite.

"They don't look very suspicious to me," said Benny. "There's a guy playing catch with a kid, a lady hanging up clothes, another lady reading some kind of magazine and a guy chopping wood."

"The guy chopping wood calls himself Potter," explained Lesage. "The other man—the one who just got hit in the face with the baseball—calls himself Vedda."

Benny looked on with interest. "Hey, Vedda's unconscious. No. No, he's up, but his nose is bleeding like mad. Now he's chasing the kid around the tent. He's stopped running...he's clutching his nose...now he's yelling at the lady who's reading the magazine...now Potter's stopped chopping wood...he's grabbing a towel from the clothesline and wetting it in the lake—good man. The towel goes on Vedda's nose...now there's someone else coming out of the tent. It's a—it's a—uh—girl. Oh yes, it's a girl..."

Lesage and Benny both leaned forward and stared as Elizabeth comforted her father, at the same time restraining him from going after Peter, who lay on the sand rolling with laughter. Neither of the spectators noticed the muffled *pop* and gurgling sound as the loosened patch gave way.

Benny was the first to feel the icy water creeping up his legs. "Hey, we're sinking!"

Lesage dropped his binoculars, took in the situation and uttered the first thing that came to mind. "Help!"

"Get in the water, grab the boat and kick towards shore," Benny ordered calmly.

Lesage's cries for help could finally be heard on shore above Mr. Vedda's moaning.

"Frank Potter, you are despicable!"

Mr. Potter looked at his wife in astonishment. "Why? What did I do?"

"You deliberately sabotaged Mr. Gee's boat by not patching it right!" Mrs. Potter accused.

"No, I didn't," he said. "Honestly. I fixed it properly."

"Then why is it sinking just now?"

"How should I know?"

"Come on, Mr. Gee!" shrieked Mrs. Vedda. "You can do it!"

"Why isn't anybody paying attention to me?" came the nasal voice of Mr. Vedda. "I'm injured!"

"Here he comes," commented Elizabeth. "The creep. And it looks like he has a sidekick—with binoculars yet!"

"Someone could have drowned, you know," Mrs. Potter was saying.

"Honestly, Mary, I—"

"Just a little farther now, Mr. Gee!" Mrs. Vedda ran into the water up to her knees, grabbed the soft yellow boat and single-handedly hauled both men ashore. "Oh, you poor dears! Quick, Elizabeth, bring blankets! Mary, start making tea!"

"Thank you," smiled Benny. "You're very kind. I'm Be—"

Gasping and sputtering, Lesage struggled to his feet. "This is—uh—uh—Dirk Brent," he puffed, staring pointedly at Benny. "He's—uh—my apprentice welder."

Slowly a look of understanding spread across Benny's face. He winked at Lesage.

"What a horrible experience for both of you!" said Mrs. Vedda.

"I don't know about that," said Elizabeth. "The important thing is, they saved the binoculars."

* * *

Bugs jogged out of the woods and into the beach campsite. "Hi, Mom. Hi, Dad. Sorry I'm late. Hey, Mr. Vedda, what happened to your face?"

Mr. Vedda mumbled something under his breath.

"He had a little accident," said Mary Potter. "Wash your hands, David. We're about to eat."

"I insist that you two stay for dinner," Mrs. Vedda was saying. "We have plenty of food. Besides, your clothes aren't completely dry yet."

"That's very nice of you," said Lesage.

Benny shuffled uncomfortably inside his blanket. "Why do we have to eat here?" he whispered. "I've got food back at the tent."

"*Shhh.* We're infiltrating."

"Oh, yeah."

They all sat down to dinner.

Mary Potter leaned over to her husband. "Remember, Frank, be nice. You've got a lot to make up for where Mr. Gee and Mr. Brent are concerned."

He sighed. "Yes, Mary. So, Mr. Gee," he began conversationally, "I understand you're a welder."

Benny looked at Lesage in wonder. "*Psst.* I thought you were an anthropologist like Uncle Vern."

Lesage cast him a meaningful glance which meant nothing to Benny. "Oh, yes, welding's my game. Dirk has been my apprentice for several months now."

"Oh, yeah," said Benny. "I'm his apprentice. I hope to be a real welder one day."

"How nice for you," said Elizabeth.

"Mr. Gee welds metal," announced Mrs. Vedda.

"And all this time I thought he welded silk," said Mr. Potter sarcastically.

He got an elbow from his wife.

"Actually, sir, I don't think you can weld silk," said Benny, really beginning to enjoy the conversation.

Lesage held his head, feeling he was losing his mind.

"So, David," began Mr. Potter, "how's your science project coming along? Did you get any more done today?"

"I put in a real tough day, Dad."

In fact, Bugs had spent the afternoon constructing his new bass drum. He had rigged a foot pedal, using a drumstick, vine and one of the springs from Mr. Vedda's tackle box, raided at lunch. Gus had contributed a buckskin blanket, which served as the material to stretch over the stump. The sound was a formidable *boom,* and Bugs loved the new drum without reservation.

"I'm dying to have a look at your work," said Mr. Potter. "What's the subject?"

"Well," began Bugs, "I don't want to say too much—I want it to be a surprise. But I will say that it has something to do with anthro—uh—"

"Anthropology?" finished Lesage breathlessly.

"Yeah," said Bugs. "That."

"It sounds very interesting," said Mr. Potter. "I'm glad to see you're taking it seriously and working hard."

"Oh, I am, Dad. I am." He could think of nothing but his drum set.

* * *

Lesage and Benny arrived back at their camp that evening just in time to hear Benny's radio beeping.

"It's Uncle Vern!" exclaimed Benny, running to answer it.

Lesage got to the radio first and switched it off.

"Aw," Benny whined, "what did you do that for? Now Uncle Vern's going to be sore at me!"

"Radio silence, remember?"

"Oh—yeah. And I bet I know why Uncle Vern suspects those people of being up to something. They sure are weird, especially that Mrs. Vedda. But when will this be over so I can call Uncle Vern?"

"Soon," Lesage promised. After all, what did it hurt to promise?

* * *

In the cafeteria of the Anthropological Museum of Ontario Dr. Vernon Sterling was standing in line waiting to pay for his coffee.

"I just can't figure out what's going on at Lake Naka-mee-chee," he said to the Director of the Geology Department. "Yesterday I sent my nephew up there with strict instructions to call in regularly, and now his radio's dead."

The geologist shrugged. "Well, you know, Benny —uh—no offense, but—"

"Okay," Sterling conceded, "so Benny's not the smartest kid in the world. But that's exactly what happened to Lesage, and he's a qualified anthropologist. And just tonight Ramsay and Hyde radioed in and demanded their equipment in a very high-handed manner. I really can't stall them much longer, but I can't help asking myself what it is they want to record and videotape, and why I can't reach the two people I sent up there." He took out his wallet and paid the cashier. "I don't fully understand it yet, but one thing is clear. Something of vast significance in the field of anthropology is taking place at Lake Naka-mee-chee."

He went to take his seat.

The cashier nudged the soup-server. "Take over for me, Lorraine. I have to make a long-distance phone call."

* * *

At the cafeteria of the Cicero Scientific Institute in Chicago, Illinois, the cashier leaned over to the Director of Anthropological Research and whispered, "I just took a call from my cousin, the cashier at the Anthropological Museum of Ontario. They've got something big under wraps at Lake Naka-mee-chee up in Canada."

"What is it?" asked the Director. His cashier was his most reliable source of inter-museum information.

The woman shrugged. "I don't know, but it's anthropology and it's big."

With a thoughtful expression on his face, the Director sat down at a nearby table.

The coffee-server nudged another employee. "Take over for me . . . "

* * *

The cashier at the cafeteria of the Museum of Anthropology in New York City dropped a little note onto the tray of the Curator of Research, who quickly sat down at an isolated table and pounced on the note. It read: *My sister-in-law at the Cicero says there's a big find in anthropology coming up at Lake Naka-mee-chee in Ontario. AMO is in on it already, so move fast.*

He put down his untouched coffee, nodded his appreciation to the cashier and hurried out of the room.

* * *

Drums now seem louder than before, noted Hyde on his pad. *Possible explanations: source has moved closer, or more drummers and drums have been added to group.* He looked up at Ramsay. "Do you think they're building towards anything?"

"We shall see," Ramsay replied. "Our need for equipment is becoming more and more urgent. Let us hope AMO will stop stalling and fill our requisition. I'm becoming aggravated with them." He opened a can of cocktail sausages. "Care for a snack?"

Hyde recoiled in contempt. "Ramsay, you have no conscience."

Ramsay produced pen and paper and began to copy Hyde's notes as the sausages warmed over the campfire. "Kindly lean back, Hyde. You're in my light."

An invitation to dinner

It was early dawn when Frank Potter rolled over in his sleeping bag. "Mary," he whispered, shaking his wife's shoulder, "do you hear anything?"

"No," she mumbled. "Go back to sleep."

"Listen—it's a plane. I'll bet Gee and Brent are leaving. Good. Maybe they got sick of sinking and being pampered by Regina."

"Shhh! You'll wake David. Go back to sleep."

Mr. Potter drifted back to sleep, but just before six he heard another plane.

"Mary, wake up. The plane's back."

"If you don't stop pestering me," she threatened, "you're going to sleep outside."

"Who could sleep with all that racket?" complained Mr. Potter, crawling out of his sleeping bag and pulling on his jogging suit. "I'm going for a run."

He stepped over the sleeping form of his son. David was apparently enjoying a good dream—his face wore a grin and his hands drummed with imaginary sticks. Mr. Potter sighed inwardly. When would the boy get off his rock music kick and become a person?

He stepped outside, gazed down the beach in the early morning haze and gaped in horror. Not only were Gee's and Brent's tents still there, but between their campsite and his own were two *new* tents. Things were going from bad to worse!

He heard a rustling behind him and turned to see Mr. Vedda, dressed and apparently ready for another day.

"Good morning, Frank."

"Oh, hi, John. Why are you up so early?"

Mr. Vedda snorted through his bandages. "I can't sleep with this tape all over my face. It's impossible to breathe. You'd think that someone would have the ingenuity to design a proper bandage, wouldn't you?"

Mr. Potter smiled sadly. "More bad news, John." A sweep of his hand indicated the new tents. "There goes our last hope of solitude."

"*Blast!*" cried Mr. Vedda.

A head poked out of one of the new tents. "Hey, you! It's six o'clock in the morning! Pipe down—you're not the only people on this beach, you know!" The head disappeared.

Mrs. Vedda's voice could be heard as she crawled through the tent opening. "What are you yelling about, dear? Is your nose giving you trouble?" She got to her feet, surveyed her surroundings and clasped her hands. "Oh, look, we have new neighbours. How nice!"

* * *

Dr. Ken Johnson of New York's Museum of Anthropology stepped out of his tent and began to build his morning campfire. In all the time he had been an anthropologist, he reflected, this was his strangest assignment. He had been sent to Lake Naka-mee-chee to find "something of great significance in the field of anthropology," but no one had been able to tell him what that something was, and the place gave no evidence of any activity other than camping. There were a few other tents, a lake and woods. Period.

Another man crawled sleepily out of a tent a few metres from his, and Johnson dropped his cooking utensils. "Oh no!" he groaned. "Not you!"

The man stared at him, eyes narrowing. "Johnson. I should have known I'd find *you* here."

"Michael Davis of the Cicero Scientific Institute. I could say I'm glad to see you, but my nose would probably grow."

"It's long enough already," growled Davis. "You're always poking it into other people's affairs. May I ask what the Museum of Anthropology is doing here?"

"That's none of your business," snapped Johnson. "And I could just as easily ask what *you're* doing here."

"And I'd answer—because I have nothing to hide —that I'm camping. This happens to be my vacation."

"Hah! Do you expect me to believe that?"

"Frankly, I'm not interested in what you believe!"

"Well, I'm camping too. What do you think of that?"

"A likely story!"

"Good morning, gentlemen," sang Mrs. Vedda as she strolled up to them, elegantly dressed in her smartest jogging suit. "I see that we're going to be neighbours. I'm Regina Vedda and I live over there." She extended her hand in greeting.

"Uh, hello," said Johnson, shaking her hand. "The name's Johnson."

"I'm Michael Davis."

"Mr. Johnson and Mr. Davis," said Mrs. Vedda. "How delightful. That other campsite over there is where Mr. Gee and Mr. Brent live. You must say hello to them."

"Mr. *who?*"

"We really must meet socially," Mrs. Vedda went on. "Maybe we can all get together with Mr. Gee and Mr. Brent—you'll like them a lot. I really must go; breakfast is being served at my camp. I just wanted to come over and make you feel welcome."

There was a long silence as Mrs. Vedda walked away. Finally Johnson said, "She's working for you, right? She's working for you and she came over to psych me out, right? Tell me I'm right!"

"I'm only here on vacation," said Davis, walking back into his tent.

* * *

While Gus sanded down a spear shaft he was working on, Bugs was reading out loud. "*Even though the Nickaninny Indians are a small tribe, they are now living all over the world and doing all sorts of different things. Some of them are doctors and lawyers and stockbrokers and accountants and things like that. One cousin even lives out on an oil rig in the Beaufort Sea, which is a drag, because the radio reception is very lousy. But most of the tribe live in*

New York, which is lucky for them because all the best rock groups tour the bigger cities.

"One of Gus's most important relatives is his Aunt Lucy, whose Nickaninny name is Babbling Brook. She is the telephone company's very best customer. If the Nickaninnies want something known, they don't use smoke signals: they tell Aunt Lucy and she does the rest. She is married to Gus's Uncle Louie, or Straight-as-an-Arrow, who had a few problems with the police last year. He was making money. Normally this is okay, but he was making it on a printing press in his basement. This is illegal in New York, so they threw poor Uncle Louie in the slammer. I wish somebody would do the same thing to the guy who ripped off our toilet."

Gus burst out laughing.

Bugs beamed. "That good, eh? Well, that's all I've got so far. Now put down that crooked stick and let's listen to some music. This is *Endomorph Live at the Toronto Harbourfront*. I was there, so this album really blows me away." He switched on the tape and grabbed his drumsticks, ready to play along. "The sound you hear at the beginning is when they catapult a flaming piano into Lake Ontario. I've got a big poster of it at home."

* * *

"Just as I suspected," said Dr. Ramsay, sitting at his radio. "I've been monitoring the calls out of this area, and these two new arrivals are American anthropologists—one from the Cicero in Chicago, and one from Anthropology in New York. Naturally they've got to go."

"How can you think of it at a time like this?" cried Hyde in great agitation. "We've just heard the ritual drumming of an undiscovered primitive civilization, and it's louder than ever!"

"Yes," said Ramsay, "and it is certainly not good policy to let two more anthropologists stay around long enough to hear it too. Johnson and Davis both have lists of achievements as long as your arm, and they're also extremely competitive. How long do you think it will be before they pounce on our discovery?"

"I'll not be party to attempted murder again!" said Hyde haughtily.

Ramsay chuckled benignly. "You do worry excessively sometimes. I have taken the liberty of pinpointing the two new gentlemen's radio frequencies. Watch this and take notes—it is true genius."

He fiddled with a dial and switched on the transmitter. "Calling Dr. Johnson. Come in, Dr. Johnson."

"Johnson here."

"Ah, yes, Johnson," said Ramsay. "I'm calling from New York on behalf of your superior. It seems there's been some sort of misunderstanding. You're at Lake Naka-mee-chee in Ontario, you say? Oh, no, no, no. You're supposed to be at Lake Talahoosie in Saskatchewan. You can't miss it—it's eight hundred kilometres due north of Moose Jaw. Well, have a good trip. Sorry for the inconvenience."

Ramsay broke the connection. "Now," he announced with glee, "we call Davis and tell him the same thing."

* * *

Ken Johnson shut off his radio and stared at it in perplexity. What could that possibly have been all about? A single thought occurred to him—Davis! Davis was trying to send him off on a wild goose chase so that the Cicero could make the discovery— whatever it was—and take all the credit. Well, it wouldn't work. Lake Talahoosie, Saskatchewan! He rushed out of his tent and burst in upon Dr. Davis, who was sitting at his radio receiving his message from Ramsay.

"Aha!" cried Johnson. "Caught in the act!"

Davis switched off his radio and wheeled. "*Me* caught in the act? Do you think you can trick me with a phony British accent?"

"I haven't forgotten the time you stranded me in Samoa!" roared Johnson. "You're not a scientist, you're—you're a sleaze!"

"And I suppose you're going to say that it wasn't you who buried my jeep in the Sahara!" bellowed Davis. "I'm not leaving! Do you hear me?"

"Well, I'm not leaving either. There's no way I'd let you and your crummy broken-down Cicero Institute beat out the Museum of Anthropology!"

"How'd you like me to beat out your teeth?"

There was a polite scratching on the side of the tent. "Yoo-hoo, gentlemen." Mrs. Vedda appeared in the doorway. "I have delightful news. We're all invited to dinner with Mr. Gee and his friend Mr. Brent at seven o'clock."

"Well," began Johnson, "I really don't think I can make it—"

"Oh, I'll be there," smiled Davis. "I can tell you all about the wonderful things we're doing at the Cicero Scientific Institute."

"It sounds fascinating," said Mrs. Vedda.

"I'll be there too," said Johnson quickly, "and I can tell you about a *real* museum—the Museum of Anthropology in New York."

"How nice," said Mrs. Vedda. "And Mr. Gee and Mr. Brent can tell us all about welding."

"It sounds extremely enjoyable," said Davis.

"I'm looking forward to it," added Johnson.

"Wonderful," said Mrs. Vedda. "Until seven o'clock, then." She left the tent.

Davis grabbed Johnson by the shoulders and pushed him out. "Until seven o'clock, then."

* * *

All eleven campers sat enjoying Benny's beef stew around Lesage's campfire. The Potters and the Veddas, tired of their strict fish diet, were especially pleased with the menu.

After one look at Elizabeth, Johnson had seated himself on her right almost as swiftly as Davis had taken the space on her left. This irked Lesage indescribably, for he had been mentally reserving her company for himself.

"Do sit down, Mr. Gee, and have some of this delicious stew." Mrs. Vedda grabbed Lesage's arm and dragged him down beside her.

"This is fantastic," said Mrs. Potter. "Mr. Brent, I must get your recipe."

"So," said Mrs. Vedda grandly, "what's new with everyone?" She looked around the fire, smiling broadly. "Mr. Johnson? How about you?"

"Oh, there's not much to tell. I'm on vacation from the extremely famous Museum of Anthropology in New York. You know—the best museum in America."

"Don't be absurd," said Davis. "Everyone knows the Cicero Scientific Institute is the finest museum in the *world*."

"Well," began Benny, resolving to uphold the reputation of the AMO, "my Uncle Vern—"

Lesage scooped up a heaping forkful of stew and jammed it into Benny's open mouth. Benny looked at him plaintively, but Lesage gestured firmly with a finger to his lips.

"Dirk talks a lot about his uncle," he explained lamely. "He owns our welding shop. Big museum-goer."

"Then he'd prefer the Cicero," decided Davis.

"Not if he has any taste," said Johnson.

"And what else is new?" prompted Mrs. Vedda.

"My dad smashed up his face," piped Peter.

"Thanks to *you*," muttered Mr. Vedda.

Mrs. Potter nudged her husband, who had been sullen and grumpy throughout dinner. "Be sociable," she said through clenched teeth.

"So," said Mr. Potter. He searched his mind, and finding no topic of conversation, said, "Tell us about the welding business, Mr. Gee."

Lesage looked stricken. "Uh—well—we use torches —welding torches, and—"

"And we weld with them," Benny supplied helpfully.

"Yes, we weld with them—things people need welded."

"All this intricate detail is making my head spin," commented Elizabeth. "I'd love some more stew if there is any."

Instantly Johnson, Davis and Lesage all jumped forward to the stew pot. They met head-on across the campfire and fell back, dazed.

Elizabeth leaned forward. "Oh, there is some left. Good." She took the spoon and helped herself to some stew.

Mary Potter turned to her son. "You're awfully quiet tonight, David."

"Well," said Bugs, "I put in a long day with my science project. I guess I'm pretty tired." In fact Bugs' mind was in the cave with his drums and Gus.

"How are you doing on that?" asked his father.

"Great!" said Bugs with enthusiasm. "I've got ten pages."

Johnson smoothed his hair. "So," he smiled at Elizabeth, "what's a nice girl like you doing in a place like this?"

"Enduring," she said coolly.

"What do you do up here for excitement?" asked Davis, refusing to be outdone by the Museum of Anthropology.

"I spend twenty-five percent of the day staring at the lake, twenty-five percent staring at the woods, twenty-five percent at the sky and twenty-five percent at the ground. I find it provides a good balance."

Frank Potter got up and stretched. "Well, I guess we'd better be going."

"But it's only eight o'clock," Mrs. Vedda protested. "The night is young."

Mary Potter smiled serenely. "Sit down, Frank."

* * *

"I can't believe it!" exclaimed Dr. Ramsay from his

tree. "Every single one of those people should be gone, but instead of leaving they're having a beach party!"

"Maybe it's a farewell party," Hyde suggested hopefully, shifting his weight on a branch. "A couple of planes will come, and by tomorrow they'll be off. And we'll be able to concentrate on our work."

"Perhaps you're right," said Ramsay skeptically. "But just in case, we'd better think of some more strategy. If they don't leave, I may have to resort to desperate measures."

Hyde looked alarmed. "What desperate measures?"

"We'll see. I haven't thought of any yet."

For a moment Hyde lost his balance, and only a frantic scramble saved him from a fall. "I trust," he panted, "that you draw the line at mass murder."

* * *

"Am I ever glad to see you!" exclaimed Gus as Bugs entered the cave a little after ten.

"Sorry I'm late, but we had to have dinner with these weird people. You wouldn't believe what they've got going back at camp! Anyway, I don't want to talk about it. Hey, something wrong, Gus?"

Gus nodded nervously. "While I was out practising spear-throwing, I caught a glimpse of somebody sneaking around the cave."

"The guy who ripped off our toilet!" exclaimed Bugs knowingly.

"I was so scared I nearly threw the spear at him— but the tip fell off. I think he must be watching the cave all the time."

"Hmm. You know, I'm starting to get a lot of bad vibes from this guy. First he takes our toilet, then he starts nosing around private property and now he's spying."

"More like haunting." Gus shuddered.

"Yeah," said Bugs, nodding thoughtfully. "We're definitely going to have to do something about him."

The purple polka-dot banner

When Frank Potter emerged from his tent to start the breakfast campfire he found Mr. Vedda waiting for him, arms folded, foot silently tapping in the sand.

"Good morning, John."

"Don't 'good morning' me. It's not a good morning. I suppose you know that there are four more tents today. What do you have to say to that?"

"*Four more?*" Mr. Potter looked down the beach and saw that there were indeed four more tents—a large one and three small ones.

"I've been doing a lot of thinking about this trip," Mr. Vedda went on coldly. "My family and I are having a miserable vacation. We're stranded in the primitive wilderness with absolutely no comforts at all, nor any of the solitude we were so confidently promised. I've decided to put the blame for this squarely where it belongs, Frank—on you."

"What are you talking about? I didn't send for these people. I'm just as upset about it as you are."

"That doesn't alter the fact that you lured us here with a false description of Lake Naka-mee-chee."

Mr. Potter flushed red. "And *you* led *me* to believe that you knew the first thing about camping—which you don't, as you prove daily."

"You defrauded us!" warned Mr. Vedda darkly.

"Sue me."

"Oh, you think I wouldn't!"

"I wouldn't put anything past you!"

Mrs. Vedda came rushing outside, struggling into her silk dressing gown. She saw her husband and his friend squared off, fists clenched, toe to toe, ready to come to blows.

"Now, now," she began sweetly.

"Stay out of this, Regina," said her husband.

"There's to be no fighting," she insisted.

"Regina, go back inside."

"I said *no fighting!*" Mrs. Vedda rushed between the two men and heaved them apart with all her might. Mr. Potter sprawled backwards and landed with a clatter in the pots and pans. Mr. Vedda sailed through the door of his tent and for a second the outline of his body could be seen in the stretched canvas at the rear. Then he bounced back out again.

Bugs helped his father up. "You know, Dad, that isn't very nice. I mean, you and Mr. Vedda are pals."

"Not anymore, we're not!" growled his father.

"Hey," said Bugs, "neighbours break up—pals don't."

Mary Potter stuck her head out of the tent. "You should listen to your son once in a while, Frank. Sometimes he's smarter than you are. Nicer too."

* * *

Bugs and Gus, concealed by thick pine needles, perched on a sturdy tree branch near the entrance to their cave. Between them they held a heavy net made of vine and weighted at the edges with stones. They had been up half the night fashioning it and now lay in wait for their prey.

"Is my dad ever going to be proud of me when I come back to camp with our toilet," Bugs whispered.

"What if the thief doesn't show?" asked Gus.

"He'll be here. He's come every day so far. And this time we'll get him."

"What if he puts up a fight?" Gus asked nervously.

"Against two Nickaninny Indians in the Nickaninny woods? He won't have a chance!"

They sat in silence for a few moments. Bugs' sensitive ears were the first to pick up a sound, the rhythm of footsteps. The two boys froze.

A figure came into view, a tall, slender young man dressed in a beige shirt and slacks and the telltale boots. His hair was sun-bleached and he had a golden tan. Creeping through the underbrush, eyes intent on the cave, he passed into the shade of the pine tree.

"*Now!*"

The net fell right onto the intruder, completely entangling him. Bugs and Gus jumped to the ground, bows and arrows trained on their prisoner.

"In the name of Chief Thundering Buffalo of the Nickaninny," announced Bugs, "you're under arrest!"

The captive struggled but only succeeded in entangling himself further. "What's going on here?"

"You know what's going on here," said Bugs. "All right, where is it?"

"Where's what?"

"The toilet you stole. Hand it over."

"I didn't steal any toilet. Let me out of this thing."

"You're only making it harder on yourself," Bugs informed him solemnly.

"Let me out! What gives you the right to attack people?"

Bugs pointed to Gus. "His dad is Chief of the Nickaninnies. That makes him the government around here. And I'm his pal."

Gus looked at him in shock.

The stranger ceased struggling. "He can't be the government around here—*I* am." He indicated a small patch on his shirt pocket which read *Department of Forestry.* "I'm the ranger."

There was an awful silence.

"He *is* the government," said Gus, nodding gloomily.

"You mean," said Bugs, "you're not the guy who ripped off our toilet? Oh, wow!"

Gus set to work cutting the prisoner free of the vine net.

"Thanks," said the ranger.

"Man, when my dad finds out I roughed up the ranger he's going to kill me!" Bugs moaned. "Hey listen, mister, we're really sorry. How about we promise never to do it again and you let us off with a warning or something?"

"There," said Gus as the ranger shrugged off the

last strands of the net. "How does that feel? Fine, I hope?"

"Yeah, thanks."

"Just a minute," said Bugs. "If you're the ranger, why do you have to sneak around in the bushes spying on people? And why do you run away every time you see us? I mean, you could just walk up and introduce yourself."

"I could, you know," said the young man thoughtfully. He flushed. "I guess I'm a little out of practice in dealing with people—in my job I never see anybody. Maybe I'd better introduce myself. Roger Forrest, Forest Ranger, that's me. And please don't laugh."

"That's a great name for a forest ranger!" Bugs exclaimed.

"Yes, my high school guidance counsellor thought so too. He sent me to forestry college by mistake."

"But you didn't have to go," said Gus.

"Well, I know, but that would have meant... " He gestured helplessly. "Anyway, I didn't have any other plans. And since I haven't seen any people for two-and-a-half years, when I heard your drums I got curious."

"Hey," said Bugs, "since you're the government here, you're the guy to talk to. I want to report the theft of a toilet."

"Hmmm, yes. The ranger does handle matters like that. I'm supposed to confirm the complaint and report the theft to my superiors, and they'll investigate and maybe implement a major search. But that would mean... " He gestured again. "Wouldn't you rather just use my toilet?"

"You have a toilet?" asked Gus.

"Of course. The one in my house."

"Gee, that's friendly," said Bugs. "I can see that you, Gus and me are going to be pals."

"Pals?"

"Right on!" said Bugs, smiling broadly. "By the way, I'm Bugs. He's Gus."

Roger processed this information. "And when a person has friends," he mused aloud, "he invites them over."

"Great," said Bugs. "I'll just get my tape deck and we'll whip on over to your place and hang out for a while. All right, let's go."

* * *

The bikini-clad Elizabeth walked out of the tent and spread a large beach towel on the sand. To her way of thinking, the sun was the only redeeming feature of Lake Naka-mee-chee, and she intended to concentrate on it and block out everything else. As she lay back with a discontented sigh, a streak of light caught her eye like a comet skimming the beach. Reflections, she told herself. Reflections off metal, glass, binoculars—*binoculars?*

The three occupants of the large newly-arrived tent, anthropologists from the D.C. Natural History Museum in Washington, had their binoculars pressed up against the windows of their tent. Ditto the three other new arrivals, representatives from The Boston Museum of Anthropology and Archaeology, the Los Angeles Historical Museum, and *L'Institut d'Anthropologie de Québec*. Lesage and Benny were out too, as were Johnson and Davis, who were trying to block each other's view.

Rigidly she stood up, wrapped herself in her towel and fled inside the Vedda tent.

Well, that was just great! Either she was being spied on by all the weirdos on the lake or she was beginning to imagine things. Not that everybody else wasn't going crazy too. Her father and Mr. Potter at each other's throats, Peter running around terrified to go near Daddy, Mother fawning over total strangers, Mrs. Potter disgusted with her husband, and Bugs, who was crazy to start with! Bugs . . .

She sat down, chin in hand. Bugs was gone all day every day, working on his project, he said. She doubted it—working on school projects in the summer was not Bugs' style. On the other hand, an interest in science might just be his way of coping with Lake Naka-mee-chee. No—impossible! Yet if Bugs were crazy to start with, maybe at Lake Naka-mee-chee he had gone suddenly sane the way everyone else had gone crazy. That thought didn't even make sense. She shook her head to clear it. This place was definitely getting to her.

"My goodness," she heard Mrs. Potter say outside, "one plane's just come in and there's another one approaching on the horizon. Frank and John won't like that."

"How wonderful!" gushed Mrs. Vedda. "More new neighbours!"

*　*　*

The ranger's residence was a small, square pre-fab cottage standing in a clearing in the dense woods two kilometres north of the cave. It had white aluminum siding with a green door and a steep roof. Roger told the boys that it also had electricity drawn from a generator in the basement. Bugs was enchanted with that immediately: electricity meant a refrigerator, and that in turn meant food. In addition, modern plumbing would be preferable to the Porta-Toilet, let alone the woods.

"So it was a real drag for both of us to have to be at Lake Nickaninny this summer," Bugs was saying as they approached the cottage. "Gus has to do his heritage and I've got to work on this dumb science project to pull my mark up to fifty. But it's a lot better now that I have some pals so I can get away from camp and the Veddas. That's why there's so much going on at the cave. Whenever I want to do anything halfway decent I have to split so my folks won't find out."

"And I was skulking around outside," said Roger sadly. "I'm sorry if I pestered you."

"Hey, pals don't pester."

Roger opened the door of the house and led them inside. The boys stared about them. All the walls were covered with framed paintings, both watercolours and oils, of varying sizes. They were hung in every available space, even in the tiny neat kitchen. Still more leaned against counters and walls as if awaiting their turn for display.

"This is beautiful," breathed Gus.

Roger looked startled. "Thank you. Uh—it is?" He looked around skeptically. "Well, maybe I got used to it after the first year or so."

"If you don't mind a little criticism," said Bugs,

"you've got a pretty small house here. You shouldn't buy so many paintings."

"Oh, I don't buy them," said Roger. "I paint them."

Gus gaped. "Really?"

Roger nodded. "Yes. And I build the frames. I find it helps pass the time. Being the ranger at Lake Naka-mee-chee isn't the most demanding job in the world, you know. You're the first people I've seen since I got here. Nothing ever happens. All I have to do is radio in once a week and say that everything's fine. The rest is spare time. Besides painting I used to take walks in the woods, but I don't do that too often anymore. Sometimes I just sit around and play my guitar."

Bugs came to life. "Guitar? Wow! I play the drums. We can jam! Let's get together tomorrow!"

"Well, I don't like to make plans too far in the future . . . "

Gus stared at him. "I thought you said you never have anything to do."

"Yeah, but . . . " Roger raised an eyebrow. "You're right. Okay, tomorrow. You know, it's great to be back in the world again. I'm in the mood for a snack. How about you guys?"

Simultaneously, Bugs and Gus snapped to attention. "Yes, please," they chorused.

* * *

Dr. Ramsay paced up and down nervously in front of his tent. "All those people!" he ranted. "And more arriving every minute. We'll never be able to chase them away—not all of them!"

Hyde breathed a sigh. It was a relief to know that

Ramsay was not planning to implement his "drastic measures." "We can focus on the Indians and get there first," he said confidently.

"Without our photographic and sound equipment we might as well get there last! And AMO obviously has no intention of sending it. It was probably the idiots at AMO who leaked the information." He paused, and his voice took on a thoughtful tone. "Then again, AMO doesn't really know what our discovery is. All they could have said is that something is happening at Lake Naka-mee-chee. Chances are all those people don't really know what they're up here for."

Hyde was suddenly interested. "Are you sure of that?"

"Not really," said Ramsay. "We'll have to devise some way to find out how much they know." He noticed the look on Hyde's face and added, "A nonviolent way, of course."

* * *

When Bugs jogged out of the woods and onto the beach late that afternoon he found his parents and Mr. and Mrs. Vedda deep in conversation over the campfire. He hoped his father and Mr. Vedda weren't fighting anymore. Mr. Vedda was kind of creepy, but they were pals, and pals shouldn't fight.

"Hi, Dad."

"Oh, hi, David."

"Hello, David," greeted Mrs. Vedda. "You're just in time to hear about this fabulous idea I've been working on." From her pocket she produced a small stack of personal stationery, removed the top sheet and read: "*You are cordially invited to attend the*

founding meeting of the Greater Lake Naka-mee-chee Tentowners' Association at 8:00 p.m. at the site of the polka-dot flag on the beach. Dress: optional."
She looked at their astonished faces. "Isn't that marvellous?"

"Regina," breathed Mrs. Potter, "what on earth are you talking about?"

"Forming a tentowners' association, of course. We form homeowners' associations at home, so why not a tentowners' association when we're living in tents? There are enough people now. It will be wonderful for adding a social air to this dreadful place."

"Regina, are you crazy?" howled Frank Potter. "You can't do that!"

"She can do whatever the heck she wants!" cried Mr. Vedda.

Oh-oh, thought Bugs.

"I'm going to deliver the invitations right away," gushed Mrs. Vedda. "Do you think I'm dressed properly for visiting?"

"You haven't been dressed properly since the day you got here!" barked Mr. Potter.

"You shut up!" cried Mr. Vedda.

"Come on." Mrs. Potter hustled her husband inside their tent. "I want to talk to you."

Mrs. Vedda set off, invitations in hand.

Elizabeth ventured outside. She was wearing her father's baggy pants and a loose-fitting shirt, sunglasses and a kerchief to hide her dark hair.

Seeing her, Bugs remembered, not without some guilt, that he had promised his father to be nice.

"Hi, Elizabeth," he said in a friendly tone. "You're looking good today."

She whipped the kerchief from her head and slapped him in the face with it. "Thanks a lot!"

"What was that for?"

"For being sarcastic!" she snarled and kept on walking.

Sheesh! thought Bugs. You try to be nice to a person . . .

*   *   *

Johnson sat in his tent staring at the invitation Mrs. Vedda had just delivered. Why would anybody bother to organize a tentowners' association? It was easily the strangest thing he'd heard of in his entire life. Was the woman crazy or what? Why should he waste his time on such a ridiculous enterprise?

Outside he heard Davis's voice. "Oh, thank you very much, Mrs. Vedda. I'll be there right at eight."

That settled it. If the Cicero Institute was going, the Museum of Anthropology was going too.

*   *   *

"You know," said Benny, "I don't like the sound of this."

Lesage, who had been delighted with the invitation because it meant an evening close to Elizabeth, looked at him. "Why?"

"Well," Benny explained, "if we're on assignment for AMO, then it's AMO's tent, and we shouldn't join any tentowners' association without getting permission from Uncle Vern. I'll go call him right now."

"Freeze!" ordered Lesage. "No Uncle Vern. All these other people have radios too, and they'd pick up your signal just like that. And if they find out what we're up to, will Uncle Vern ever be mad!"

Benny hung his head. "Yeah—okay."

Lesage rubbed his hands together gleefully. Tonight for sure he'd have Elizabeth all to himself. Who else would go to something as ludicrous as a tentowners' association meeting?

* * *

In the large tent housing three Washington anthropologists, a heated debate about Mrs. Vedda's invitation was raging.

"This really makes me nervous," said the head of the group. "I've never seen anything like it before."

"Yes, but what does it mean?" asked the second member of the expedition.

"Maybe that crazy lady really is forming a tentowners' association. It's possible."

"Oh yeah, sure! For what purpose? To ask the government for sidewalks?"

"Quit squabbling," said the leader. "This could be something cooked up by another museum to throw us off the track. But maybe by going we'll find out something to put us *on* the track. We're going."

"That's insane."

"Well," said the third, "we shouldn't really worry about being put off the track, because we don't actually know what we're looking for anyway. We have nothing to lose."

* * *

The inhabitants of Lake Naka-mee-chee turned out in full force for the founding meeting of the Greater Lake Naka-mee-chee Tentowners' Association. Curiosity had won out over mistrust, and every camper was there, gathered around the broom Mrs. Vedda had stuck in the ground. A purple polka-dot silk scarf flew from it. Under the flag stood a small folding table at which Mrs. Vedda sat, a serene expression on her face.

Lesage was most dismayed. He had expected that he and Benny would be the only ones there. Now it would be impossible for him to get very close to Elizabeth.

In the crowd Johnson kept a sharp eye on Davis, Davis kept a sharp eye on Johnson, and all the recently-arrived anthropologists looked around nervously, keeping sharp eyes on each other.

Near the front Frank Potter stirred restlessly. "I can't believe the stupidity of all this!" he growled. "How could I allow this to happen?"

Elizabeth looked around uncomfortably. Her mother had insisted that she wear her own clothes rather than her father's, and she had succeeded in finding a shapeless track suit. So far no one was staring at her. Soon night would fall and she could melt into the shadows. She sighed. What a horrible experience it was to have to sit and watch one's mother make a fool of herself!

Bugs, too, was restless. All he wanted to do was get away from camp and be with Gus and Roger. There didn't seem to be much of a chance to escape at the moment, as he was under his mother's watchful eye.

As Mrs. Vedda rapped for silence Dr. Ramsay snaked his way out of the woods and hid behind the Veddas' tent. It was important to overhear what was said at this gathering.

"Good evening, neighbours," Mrs. Vedda began. "I'm Regina Vedda. Welcome to the founding meeting of the Greater Lake Naka-mee-chee Tentowners' Association. I've been here for over a week now, and it has become increasingly clear to me that we need some good community involvement."

There was dead silence.

Mrs. Vedda beamed. "Before we start with the business, let me introduce my party. The gentleman with the gray shirt and the bandaged nose is my husband, John. The little boy beside him is my son, Peter. And the young lady in the track suit is my daughter, Elizabeth."

All eyes turned to Elizabeth, and an enormous cheer rose from the crowd.

Mrs. Vedda was smiling. This was going even better than she'd hoped. "And that lovely family over there are our friends, the Potters." She waited for the cheer, but none came so she went on. "The first item on the agenda is to select the association officers. First we need a president. Are there any nominations from the floor?"

There was an embarrassed murmur, then a voice from the back piped up, "You do it, lady!"

"Oh, me? How flattering. Any other nominations? No? Well, that's wonderful, then. I seem to be acclaimed. How nice. All right, now we need a vice-president. Nominations?"

There was complete silence, then the same voice from the back called out, "You do it, lady!"

"Oh, well," said Mrs. Vedda. "I suppose I could handle the president's and the vice-president's positions. But we do need a secretary."

This time a chorus of voices: "You do it, lady!"

"Oh, well, I guess I can be secretary too," said Mrs. Vedda, secretly delighted to have been given this vote of confidence. "And finally we'll need a social director."

Now almost everyone chorused, "You do it, lady!

"Oh, very well," said Mrs. Vedda. "And as social director I declare our first social event of the season." There was an uncomfortable stir. "Tomorrow evening at exactly seven o'clock, right here under the polka-dot tentowners' flag, there will be a big fish fry and bonfire. It promises to be a most successful event and a wonderful time for all. And don't forget, it's B.Y.O.F."

"What's B.Y.O.F. lady?" called the voice.

"Bring Your Own Fish." She beamed. "So we'll all see each other out on the lake tomorrow. Now, could I have an idea of how many of you are planning to attend?"

Mr. Vedda put his hand up, followed by Peter and Mrs. Potter, who nudged her husband, causing him to raise his. Bugs, who had not been paying attention, put up his hand because everyone else did so. When Davis raised his hand, Johnson did too. Then Mrs. Vedda glared at her daughter and Elizabeth finally raised her hand. Instantly everyone else jumped on the bandwagon.

Mrs. Vedda counted hands. "One hundred percent attendance! That's wonderful. And by tomorrow we may even have some new members. Now I'm leaving the floor open to any other business. Does anyone have anything to say?"

"Something to say!" shouted the voice at the

back. "We want shorter meetings!"

"All right, then," said Mrs. Vedda. "This meeting is adjourned. But you don't have to go now. Elizabeth is serving tea."

The tea table was mobbed.

* * *

Dr. Ramsay walked into his camp, his eyes wide, his face registering deep shock.

Hyde was alarmed. "Are you all right? What happened?"

"I—I don't know," replied Ramsay, shaking his head. "It looked to me like all those anthropologists —each one of them after our discovery—were banding together and forming—they formed a tentowners' association!"

Hyde stared at him. "A what?"

"A tentowners' association! This lady, Mrs. Vedda, one of the women in the first group of campers, came out and ran the whole thing. She organized a fish fry!"

"A fish fry?"

"Yes. And we're going to it tomorrow night to keep an eye on things."

"But we'll be seen!" Hyde protested. "We could be recognized!"

"We'll disguise ourselves and we won't slip in until it starts to get dark. You know, Hyde, I'm not sure about this, but I think it's possible that this Mrs. Vedda could deserve a medal. She's got all those anthropologists so confused that they don't know what to do except participate in her social events. They'll be fishing all day and partying all night, and that keeps them out of the woods and away from our Indians. Hyde, we may just pull this off after all!"

"So why do you look so worried?"

"It's not worry so much as shock. Frankly, Hyde, I'm not sure I can believe what I witnessed! That Vedda woman ... Anyway, tonight we'll call AMO and remind them about our equipment."

"Do you think they'll send it?" asked Hyde.

"We'd better hope so."

Gone fishing

The small Air Northland office was a beehive of activity.

"I don't understand it," said the airline's president to his secretary. "I just don't understand it! Why all of a sudden does everyone want to go to Lake Naka-mee-chee?"

"Camping is very popular nowadays," she said soothingly. "And I understand Lake Naka-mee-chee is a beautiful spot."

"There are a thousand identical spots! Over the past twenty years we've flown an average two-sevenths of a person per year to Naka-mee-chee. Now we're making five or six daily flights and we still can't keep up."

"Perhaps it's word of mouth. If some campers like it, they tell their friends."

"That brings us to the most confusing part," said the president, his voice rising in pitch. "Except for that party of seven that went up a little over a week ago, everyone else is from a museum. Why do museums suddenly want to send their people up to the back of beyond? They're starting to come from all over the world—England, Germany, France. Why, just this morning we flew up a pair from Japan!"

"Well, maybe there's something that interests them up there."

"Impossible. Take my word for it, Gina, there's nothing at Lake Naka-mee-chee. Nothing at all."

* * *

Elizabeth Vedda was up early, unable to sleep because of her father's snoring, which had been much worse since he had caught Peter's baseball in the face. She dressed quickly and stepped out of the tent into the cool morning air. Perhaps at this hour she could move about without being the target of all those binoculars.

With a yawn she counted all the new tents. There were five. And yes, an airplane on the horizon. Idly she wondered why all these people were coming to Lake Naka-mee-chee. She winced visibly—no doubt her mother would personally greet the new arrivals and draft them into the Tentowners' Association. She glanced over to where the polka-dot banner proudly flew from the broom handle. Below it sat the Association's suggestion box—Elizabeth had a few suggestions, but she would try to keep them to herself.

Hearing sounds behind her, she turned to see Bugs tiptoeing carefully out of the Potters' tent.

"Good morning, Bugs."

"Good morning, Elizabeth." Bugs was a trifle wary. The last time he had said anything to her she had hit him.

"Where are you off to so early in the morning?"

Bugs patted his notebook. "I'm going to do some more work on my science project."

"Bugs, don't give me that. I know just as well as you that even the greatest science student in the world—which you obviously aren't—wouldn't spend this much time on a science project. Where do you go all the time?"

Bugs shrugged. "Around. Out in the woods. You know, making observations for my project."

Elizabeth snatched at the notebook. "I'd like to read that."

Bugs held it away from her. "No one's seeing it until it's finished," he said. "Now I've got to go. I'm late for—uh—making observations. Tell my folks I'll be back for lunch." He ran off into the woods.

Elizabeth watched him go until she was distracted by a familiar voice behind her.

"Oh, how delightful! New neighbours!"

* * *

"I really appreciate your letting me hang some of my paintings in here," said Roger, putting up one last landscape in a space near the cave entrance.

Bugs stepped back and looked at the cave walls critically. Rows of paintings hung on all sides as far as the light stretched, leaving hardly any cave visible. "It's a real improvement," he decided. "It gives the place—you know—atmosphere."

Gus laughed and reached up to straighten a landscape. "Yeah. The atmosphere of Roger's place."

"Okay," said Bugs. "Enough art. Roger, let's play some music."

Roger picked up the guitar he had brought along with the paintings. "It's not the greatest, Bugs. I picked it up for eight dollars at a garage sale when I was twelve."

Bugs shrugged. "Well, the drums aren't exactly the Endomorph Boom Factory either. Let's give it a try."

Roger began with a slow blues number, which Bugs enhanced with a heavy beat.

Gus was impressed. They hadn't even practised, but it was coming out music!

"Faster!" called Bugs.

Roger switched to a faster, more complicated chord pattern, and Bugs swung into a rock beat. His powerful and confident drumming inspired Roger to experiment a little and he picked up the tempo to a wilder rhythm.

Gus was staring in amazement. Twenty-four hours ago Bugs had placed the ranger under arrest. Now they were playing as though they had been partners for years.

Bugs broke pattern and flew into a solo. Roger caught up, chording expertly, and Bugs ended the number with a crash of the pot-lid cymbal.

Gus applauded earnestly. "That was fantastic! You guys are really good!"

"He's right, you know," said Bugs, flushed with pleasure. "We're okay. Obviously it would sound better with better instruments, but under the circumstances we're amazing!"

Roger was glowing. "It's been a long time since I've done anything like that. Come to think of it, I've *never* done anything like that. Bugs, you're a tremendous drummer. It's too bad Gus doesn't play anything."

"Well, actually," said Gus, "I do have a little

native flute in my knapsack." He rummaged through his things and pulled out a wood-carved fife about the length of a clarinet.

Bugs was appalled. "You mean, with the great sounds going down here all week you had an instrument and didn't jam? Are you crazy or something?"

"But Bugs, with the type of music you play—"

"Any instrument can play great rock," Bugs insisted. "Let's hear the sound."

Gus put the flute to his mouth and played a few experimental notes.

"Great sound!" Bugs raved. "All right, let's play!"

"Hold it, Bugs. I only know a few tunes. I don't know what you're playing."

"You don't have to know the song. Just listen to the music, really get into it and shoot for Jupiter."

Roger strummed some introductory chords and Bugs threw himself at the drums. Gus sat staring at his flute.

"Play something!" ordered Bugs, not interrupting his drumming.

Gus put the flute to his lips and hesitantly played a note. It was wrong, he was certain. But wait—a little higher maybe. He tried again.

"Right on!" cheered Bugs, his drumming thunderous.

"Right on!" shouted Roger.

"Right on!" Gus echoed. He put the flute back to his mouth and blew his brains out. He was making it to Jupiter—or at least well past the Bronx!

The high, piercing notes of the flute cut the air, melding with the guitar and drums, inspiring the three to play harder and louder. Gus grew more and more creative, sprinkling the piece with small trills and the occasional red-hot wail. Roger strummed heavily, switching the lead back and forth with Gus. Bugs was just a blur, drumming like a madman. They played louder and louder, faster and faster, until perspiration glistened on the faces of all three. Then Bugs lapsed into a devastating roll and hit the bass drum twice in preparation for a final crescendo. They crashed to a triumphant finish and collapsed backwards, cheering themselves hoarse.

"Wow!" exclaimed Bugs joyously, wiping the sweat from his brow. "We are amazing! We're monstrous!"

Gus and Roger nodded enthusiastically.

"Do you know what?" cried Bugs hoarsely. "We're a group. Do you hear that? A *group!*"

Roger and Gus stared at him.

"We're good enough to be a rock group, and I've got the perfect name for us! *The Nickaninny!*" He gestured grandly and hit the cymbal for effect.

"Great, Bugs," said Gus, "but maybe we'd better—"

"We'll rehearse all day and all night," raved Bugs, his enthusiasm still at fever pitch. "I can teach you all the best music—Endomorph, Migraine, Busted Chandelier, The Glob, Dim Bulb, The Behinds, Plankton, Flaming Sidewalks, Nuclear Teacup! Wow!" He reached forward to hit the drums for emphasis and accidentally caught a glimpse of his watch. "Oh-oh. I'm forty-five minutes late for lunch. I'll be back, you guys, as soon as I can get away. We've got a lot of work to do today!" He ran off in the direction of the beach.

Roger looked worried. "Exactly what does being part of this group entail?"

Gus shrugged, laughing. "I have no idea. I guess only Bugs knows, and maybe even he doesn't. I'm sure you've noticed that our pal makes up life as he goes along. Anyway, it won't be dull."

*　*　*

Dr. Ramsay paced up and down in front of his tent. "I *knew* we shouldn't have come to Lake Naka-mee-chee without bringing a few disguises along! Now how are we going to sneak into that party without being recognized?"

"It was an understandable oversight, Ramsay," said Hyde in an abstracted tone.

The music that day had been overpowering. In addition to drums, several new instruments were audible. He was making extensive notes on what he had heard, but had given up trying to interest Ramsay in it. The man was too obsessed with cloak-and-dagger to be aware of anything else.

"How come the road to fame has to be so complicated?" muttered Ramsay. "Is it too much to ask that I be allowed to make a simple momentous discovery without having to keep track of scores of intruders at the same time?"

"Maybe we shouldn't go at all," Hyde suggested hopefully.

"Nonsense! We'll go after dark, wear hats down over our faces, pull our collars up high and stay away from the campfire. No one will recognize us."

*　*　*

The Vedda family, Mr. Vedda at the oars, moved

out to the middle of the lake and set their lines to fish.

Mrs. Vedda clasped her hands with joy. "It's so wonderful! Everyone is out catching fish for to-night's party."

It was true. Lake Naka-mee-chee was speckled with a multitude of dinghies as the entire Tentowners' Association, including the newly-drafted members who had arrived that morning, were out busily fishing to fill the frying pans for the fish fry.

Elizabeth noticed with relief that although they had all brought their binoculars along they were too busy spying on each other to pay much attention to her.

Johnson cast a calculating look at Davis to check on his progress: there was no way the Cicero Institute was going to outfish the Museum of Anthropology!

"Good work!" called Mrs. Vedda to a man who had just reeled in a big trout. She smiled blissfully. "Now *this* is what I call camping!"

* * *

As darkness fell the first annual Greater Lake Naka-mee-chee Tentowners' Association fish fry was getting underway. While the president delivered her welcoming address, a grumbling Frank Potter was building up the fire, helped by his son. The two were both working under protest. Bugs was not interested in the camp activities, not having spent very much time there himself. The Nickaninny was the only thing on his mind: the group had spent the entire afternoon rehearsing his favourite numbers until

Roger and Gus inexplicably asked for a rest. Bugs could hardly wait to do more the next day.

Meanwhile Elizabeth, assigned to the duty of cleaning the day's catch, was fighting off a multitude of volunteer helpers. Johnson and Davis, who had managed to hold each other to a 0-0 tie in the fishing, were bickering and holding up examples of their filleting handiwork for judgment. The two gentlemen from the London Historical Museum were claiming fish-cleaning supremacy on the grounds that they were British. A representative from the State Anthropological Museum in Moscow was demonstrating Russian fish-cleaning expertise, and a Japanese anthropologist was quoting figures on the percentage of fish in an average Japanese diet. Benny was asserting that Canada had the best fishing in the world, but no one was paying any attention to him.

Elizabeth held her head. "This is a fish fry, not an international incident! Quit squabbling and clean!"

Frank Potter appraised his fire. "It'll be ready soon." He shook his head. "I feel like such a darn fool, participating in this—association!"

"Gee, Dad, I guess you're not having a very good vacation."

"That's for sure. We never should have brought those Veddas along."

"I could have told you that," said Bugs.

"And all these people! I can't understand where they're coming from! I've got a good mind to pack it all up and go home as soon as we can get a flight!"

Bugs was aghast. "You can't do that!"

His father looked at him. "Why not?"

"Well—uh—I—er—I haven't finished my science project yet."

Mr. Potter looked at his son accusingly. "Don't tell me you *like* it here?"

"No!" said Bugs quickly. "But, I mean, I'm really counting on pulling my science mark up to fifty. Why, my project is so good, they might even give me fifty-five!"

"Say, when can I read that, David?"

"Soon, Dad. It's not finished yet."

They soon advanced to the eating stage. On the menu, along with fish, was an excellent variety of canned vegetables. Mrs. Vedda had extorted these from the supplies of various members of the Tentowners' Association. Although none of the contributors had any sort of enthusiasm for the association or its president, each had found it impossible to say no to her. They were all sure that Mrs. Vedda had to be more than she seemed. It might very well be beneficial, then, to be on her good side.

Ramsay and Hyde stood scouting at the edge of the trees.

"Okay," said Ramsay, "remember: collar up, hat down, stay away from the fire. Try to find out how much these people know."

They darted out from the trees, went around the Veddas' tent and eased themselves into the crowd. Almost immediately Mrs. Vedda was upon them.

"Oh, hello there. Don't you have any food?" She grabbed them both by the arm and dragged them over to the bonfire, where she heaped up two plates with fish and vegetables.

"Uh—I'm not really very hungry," said Ramsay,

turning his face away from the firelight.

"Of course you are!" said Mrs. Vedda. "You had a big afternoon fishing."

She jammed the plates into both men's chests. "Now," she said, leading them back to the party, "you sit down right here and have a good time." She walked away, leaving them in a small group.

"So," said Ramsay conversationally to the group in general, "how is it going with everybody?"

The answer was an unenthusiastic chorus of "okays" and "all rights." A man who had accidentally abandoned ship earlier that afternoon sneezed.

"Come, come, gentlemen," said Ramsay. "Let's have no pretense among us. We all know what we're here for. It's hardly disloyal to our respective employers to compare notes a little."

This created an uncomfortable stir.

Finally a man from Detroit spoke. "I don't really know what I'm doing. I was just told to come up here and not miss out on whatever happens."

"Moi aussi," said a Frenchman. "Does not anyone know what is really happening here?"

Reluctantly, all admitted that they didn't know what they were looking for. Ramsay looked meaningfully at Hyde. From this lot, anyway, they had found out what they wanted to know.

Regina Vedda was at her hostessing best, drifting from group to group, generating small talk and making sure that everyone had had enough to eat.

Mary Potter sat by the fire sipping tea and reflecting that she was thoroughly disgusted with both sides of an argument. She felt sorry for her husband, though. Frank was really disappointed in his dream holiday. It was nice of David to spend this evening with his father. David was a nice boy, even though she was sure he was spending all his time somewhere out in the woods listening to his tape deck. After finding that half the clothes she had packed for him were missing, she assumed he had replaced them with his portable stereo. Normally she would have said something, but Frank was already so unhappy about this holiday she didn't dare make things worse. As long as David came up with some semblance of a science project, the trip wouldn't be a total loss for Frank.

* * *

At Roger's cottage Gus stood dressed in full Naka-mee-chee regalia—including war axe—trying to hold a stop-action pose. Roger was painting him, improvising the native setting in the background. It was not necessary to go outside: in his two-and-a-half years as resident ranger Roger had memorized Lake Naka-mee-chee and its environs.

"I really appreciate this," said Gus, momentarily losing his balance and steadying himself against the wall. "If my father likes it he may not notice that I fudged the war mask."

"Let's take a break," Roger decided. They moved to the kitchen and Gus accepted a Coke. Roger picked up the notebook that Bugs had forgotten to take back to camp. "I'm interested in this project Bugs talks so much about. Do you think he'd mind if I took a look?"

Gus laughed. "He'd be pleased. Help yourself."

Roger leafed through the pages. "He's certainly written a lot." He picked a sample section and read aloud: *"One of the less boring Nickaninny cousins is Albert, Brown Beaver. He was the first guy to parachute off the top of the Empire State Building and live. For this he got put on probation, which he violated when his pet boa constrictor got loose in Bloomingdale's. He was killed. (Not Albert—the snake.)"* Roger flipped a few pages. *"Sometimes on Saturdays the Nickaninnies go to the theatre. They never go to rock concerts, which I don't think is very smart because there are always so many great groups in New York . . . "* He looked up in awe. "*This* is his science project?"

"Yup. This is it."

"But he'll fail!"

"He failed already. This is the make-up."

Roger looked stricken. "But . . . " he gestured helplessly with both hands.

"Don't worry about Bugs," said Gus. "He'll land on his feet."

"He's odd," commented Roger. "What does he mean when he says 'Nickaninny'? I want to paint the group name on the bass drum, but I can't figure out what we're called."

"I think we're The Nickaninny. It's the way Bugs says Naka-mee-chee."

"Oh," said Roger. "Then we must be The Naka-mee-chee."

"I don't think so."

"No?"

"No."

"Oh, then if we're not The Naka-mee-chee we must be The Nickaninny—which means Naka-mee-chee but really isn't. That's logical, isn't it?"

Gus laughed. "Now you're starting to think like Bugs."

What you can find in the woods

Elizabeth Vedda stepped out of her tent, stretched in the morning sunshine and sighed. Idly she took note of a few new tents—she wasn't quite sure how many because by this time it was impossible to keep track. Lack of interest was also a factor.

A book tucked under her arm, she walked a little way into the woods, found a shady tree, sat down and began to read.

She had been there for twenty minutes when she heard light footsteps on the pine needles and looked up to see Bugs making his way through the woods. He passed quite close, walking purposefully, oblivious of her presence.

As she stood behind a tree and watched his disappearing back, a sudden impulse came over her. Why not follow him? Then maybe she'd find out where he'd been spending his days. As quietly as she could, she set out after Bugs, keeping him in sight but never too close. He was not hard to track. If he disappeared she could still follow the sound of his unguarded footsteps and the soft drumming on his leg.

She followed him for a while and then watched with wide eyes as he stepped through brush and seemed to disappear. Elizabeth squinted. It was the entrance to a cave. She waited behind a bush for a few minutes, but when Bugs did not come out she slowly edged her way forward.

* * *

Dr. Ramsay's face wore an expression of deep satisfaction. "All those anthropologists out there—the best scientific minds from all over the world, and none of them with any idea what they're looking for! How beautiful!"

Hyde was uneasy. "One of these days they're bound to hear the Indians, and then we'll have competition."

"Not really," said Ramsay, "because they don't have enough time to puzzle out what's going on. First of all, that Mrs. Vedda is keeping them busy twenty-four hours a day, and that's just making them suspicious of her and of each other. If they do have any spare time they spend it making advances to her daughter. And they only have forty-eight hours."

"What are you talking about?"

Ramsay grinned triumphantly. "Listen carefully. We've both been hearing the tribal music, and even though we can't hear it very well, it's obviously of a religious nature. And it's being played with greater intensity at uneven intervals day by day. But the ceremony is building. I believe it is building towards an important religious ritual which will take place tomorrow night."

Hyde scoffed. "I suppose you're going to tell me what time tomorrow night!"

"Indeed I am. It will begin sometime between 11:06 p.m. and 1:09 a.m."

"How could you possibly know that?"

"Because tomorrow night there will be a lunar eclipse," announced Ramsay. "And what is left of the Naka-mee-chee tribe will be here in force to celebrate it."

Hyde leapt to his feet. "Ramsay, that's brilliant! I forgive you all your ridiculous antics!"

Ramsay smiled triumphantly. "Now the thing to do is secure our equipment."

"How do you know they'll send it? There's a time factor involved now."

"They'll send it," Ramsay promised grimly. "Listen."

He sat down at the radio and homed in on AMO's frequency. "Dr. Sterling, please. At once." There was a pause, then, "Dr. Sterling, it's Dr. Ramsay at Lake Naka-mee-chee. Look here, Sterling, I'll be blunt. This place is crawling with anthropologists from all over the world. We are on the verge of a major discovery and so far only Hyde and I know what it is. If our equipment is not airlifted in by tomorrow morning, Hyde and I will resign immediately and AMO will be cut completely out of the discovery. That is all I have to say. Good day."

He switched the radio off before Sterling could reply. "There," he said confidently. "The thought of a discovery being made in Ontario without AMO will set him scurrying."

* * *

Bugs found Gus and Roger in the shadows at the rear of the cave, adding more paintings to the already cluttered decor.

"Hi, guys. Hey, this is a nice one, Roger. Too bad it's of Lake Nickaninny."

"Hi, Bugs. How was your fish fry?"

"Oh, man, did it stink! It was—"

With a *click,* the tape deck erupted with the sounds of *The Itch Live in Concert.*

Gus stiffened with shock. "The alarm!"

"It's the *real* guy who ripped off our toilet!" Bugs exclaimed. "Quick!"

Shocked by the sudden noise, Elizabeth tumbled into the cave entrance and looked up in terror as three menancing figures advanced toward her from the shadows. One carried a bow and arrow, one a large spear and the third a battle-axe. She opened her mouth to scream, then gaped. The one in the middle was none other than . . .

"Bugs Potter, what is this?"

All three attackers dropped their weapons with a clatter.

"Oh—uh—hello, Elizabeth."

"What is this place? The Ritz?"

"Uh—it's just a cave. I found it when I was doing my project."

"All these paintings?"

Bugs cringed. "They're good, aren't they?"

"Where did they come from?" Her eyes scoured the room. "And where did you get all those chocolate bars?"

"It's amazing what you can find in the woods."

"You—you're living here in the lap of luxury

while we sit in the sand watching our fathers fight! Eating chocolate bars while we starve in misery on the beach! How could you? I always knew you were a creep but I didn't know you were despicable!"

"Uh—I guess everyone's entitled to an opinion," Bugs mumbled.

"You are a miserable excuse for a human being!" she seethed. "You're a worm!"

Bugs turned to his two friends. "Isn't anybody going to defend me?"

"Yes, well—excuse me, Miss," piped up Roger, "but I don't think you should—"

"Mind your own business!" snapped Elizabeth.

"Sorry," he mumbled.

She spread her hands, indicating the cave. "You've got everything here! I suppose you've got our Porta-Toilet too!"

"Oh, no," said Gus. "That's gone. I mean, gone for real."

"Who are these two creeps anyway?"

Bugs pointed to his two friends in turn. "Gus, Roger—remember I was telling you guys about the Veddas? Well, this is Elizabeth."

"*This* is Elizabeth?" gasped Gus.

"Elizabeth Vedda?" echoed Roger.

Elizabeth had caught sight of Bugs' drum set. "Aha! Our pots! And Mother's pants! And her vest! Bugs Potter, you are low! The nerve of you, taking our things and—" She stared at the newly-painted bass drum. "*The Nickaninny?*"

"That's our rock group," announced Roger proudly.

"Your *what?*" She ignored Roger and stared at

Bugs expectantly.

"There was nothing to do up here, so we formed a rock group."

"When our families hear about this," shrilled Elizabeth, "they'll throw you in the lake and hold you under!"

"They don't have to know," said Bugs pleadingly.

"Oh, yes they do, Bugs Potter! I owe you that much!"

"Can't we talk about this?" asked Bugs weakly.

"Why should I have anything to say to you?" she demanded.

"Well," Roger offered shakily in the strained silence, "I baked a cake last night. Why don't we all discuss it at my house over a cup of tea?"

"That's a sick joke!" said Elizabeth. "I see your friends are just like you, Bugs."

"He does have a house," said Gus. "Wait'll you see it!"

"Yeah," added Bugs, desperately trying to stall Elizabeth. "It even has plumbing!"

* * *

Bugs, Gus and Roger sat at the ranger's kitchen table having seconds of chocolate cake while Elizabeth soaked in a hot bath, her first in over a week. She had been overjoyed beyond belief to find that such a facility existed in Roger's house and had almost wept when he offered her the use of it.

"She won't appreciate it," Bugs was saying. "She'll just stroll right out of here and start opening her big mouth again. She'll squeal to my dad, and The Nickaninny will be finished."

"Gee, Bugs," said Roger, "when you described Elizabeth Vedda you gave us the impression she was homely."

"So?" said Bugs.

The ranger dropped his voice to a whisper. "She's beautiful!"

Bugs' jaw dropped. "She is?"

Gus and Roger nodded.

"Well, you've got to admit she's mean," said Bugs.

"Not really," said Roger. "And she has a lovely voice."

They listened to Elizabeth singing joyously as she splashed.

Bugs snorted. "That's not singing!"

"You know," said Gus, "we could really use a lead singer for The Nickaninny."

Bugs opened his eyes wide. "You mean *Elizabeth?*"

"I think she'd be really good at our material," said Roger.

"Aw! We can't do that. She'd spoil the group!"

"Why?"

"Well—because she's Elizabeth! The Nickaninny is important, and Elizabeth is Elizabeth!"

They heard her pull the plug to empty the tub.

"Listen, Bugs," said Gus, "if she's a member of the group there's no way she's going to go home and tell your parents. It's our only chance to keep The Nickaninny together."

"She'll never buy it," Bugs managed weakly.

"Just try," Roger urged.

"*Me?* Why don't *you* ask her?"

"You're the group leader," said Gus.

"Aw, I don't want to ask her!"

"Ask me what?" said Elizabeth, towelling her wet hair as she walked into the room.

Bugs cleared his throat. "Elizabeth, you wouldn't want to join The Nickaninny, would you?"

"We need a lead singer," added Roger shyly.

"And we heard you in the bath," put in Gus. "You're great."

Elizabeth considered the proposal. What else was there to do? Besides, she could tell by the expression on Bugs' face that he was hoping she'd say no. "Yes," she replied instantly.

"Yes what?" asked Bugs.

"Yes, I want to be your lead singer."

"Oh, but you'll hate it, Elizabeth," Bugs protested. "You know how you hate all my music. Well, we're playing only the very best—which is the very worst for you, you know." He looked at her. "Right?"

"I love you too, Bugs," she smiled sweetly.

Bugs looked at Gus and Roger. "She's being mean to me again!"

"It's settled then," said Gus.

"Not yet!" cried Bugs, jumping to his feet. "The lead singer of The Nickaninny has to be qualified. Elizabeth, let's hear you scream."

"Okay." Using all the breath control she had acquired in her long conservatory training, Elizabeth filled her lungs and let out a high-pitched, blood-curdling scream that lasted ten seconds. "How's that?"

Gus and Roger were cringing back in their chairs, eyes popping.

Bugs, on the other hand, wore an expression of pleased interest. "Hey," he said, "that's pretty good. Let's go back to the cave and have a rehearsal." He looked at Elizabeth. "We'll do some Endomorph."

"Gezundheit," she said.

* * *

When Ramsay returned to the campsite after burying some garbage, he found Hyde on his usual listening rock, his face white.

"Listen, Ramsay!" he barely whispered. "They've added something new—women screaming!"

Ramsay listened carefully. "It sounds awfully violent," he commented.

"Is there anything in our study to indicate that these people practised human sacrifice?"

"Of course not," said Ramsay. "Their religion couldn't be anything like that. Though it is rather—chilling, mind you."

"That is definitely the sound of a soul in torment," Hyde insisted, shivering.

"Shhh. Listen."

* * *

Another rehearsal of The Nickaninny, this time with Elizabeth Vedda on lead vocal, started that morning and extended to encompass the whole afternoon.

Elizabeth yowled out the lyrics to Endomorph's first big hit, "Electric Guitarist on the Roof," as Bugs, Gus and Roger crashed, shrilled and strummed along. They barrelled through to a big finish.

Bugs glowed with pleasure. "Wow! I have to admit it—since *she* joined, the group is better than ever!"

Elizabeth was breathless but happy. For some reason she had enjoyed screaming her lungs out singing those terrible rock songs Bugs was teaching the group. It was an exhausting experience, and yet she hadn't felt so relaxed in days. Perhaps this was an outlet for her frustration over being stuck at Lake Naka-mee-chee. She wished Gee, Brent, Johnson, Davis and the rest of the binocular brigade could see her.

"Wow, Elizabeth," said Gus, "you sure are fantastic!"

"You're a remarkably quick study," added Roger. "You learned all the lyrics in no time at all, and you've got a really good ear for tune."

"What tune?" Elizabeth scoffed.

"Hey!" said Bugs, inadvertently slamming the bass drum as he spoke. "Shut up! I don't want to hear any more cracks about Endomorph!"

"Oh, Bugs, don't be so sensitive. When you talk about rock music you sound like my mother talking about her Tentowners' Association!"

Bugs turned to Gus and Roger. "You see? Look how mean she is!"

"Calm down, Bugs," soothed Gus. "Remember, Elizabeth is a member of the group, right?"

"Yeah," conceded Bugs unhappily. "But—she doesn't even respect our music!"

"I respect rock," argued Elizabeth, her eyes shining with sincerity. "I understand the deeper structures in the lyrics and the beautiful counter-melodies of the music. I realize that rock musicians are artists who can truly have an effect on human destiny, and I am grateful for their significant contribution to humanity."

"Do you really mean that?" asked Bugs.

"No."

Bugs stared in outrage at Gus and Roger. He pointed at Elizabeth and mouthed the words "You see?" but no sound came out.

* * *

Elizabeth was having a wonderful day. She'd had a hot bath and a shampoo, she'd joined a rock group, she was driving Bugs crazy—a great day indeed. She'd also read Bugs' project, so she'd had a good laugh too. In fact, she was still laughing as she and a somewhat less jubilant Bugs arrived at the Potter-Vedda campsite just before suppertime.

Instantly a crowd was upon them.

"Where have you been?" stormed Davis. "I've been worried sick!"

"I've been worried sicker!" shouted Johnson.

"You should really have told us you were going to be out for the day," said Lesage reproachfully.

"Something could have happened to you," put in one of the Russians.

Two anthropologists from Hong Kong spoke solemnly to her in Cantonese.

She smiled blissfully. "Good evening, all."

As she and Bugs walked towards their campfire the whole mass followed.

"And I say we at the Cicero Institute were more worried than you at the Museum of Anthropology!"

"Shut up, Davis!"

Peter Vedda pranced up to his sister. "Hi, Elizabeth. Dad went out looking for you in the woods, you know, and we all had to go out and find him. Mr. Potter said Dad sat in poison oak. Mr. Potter laughed. I did too. Dad's real mad."

"Hi, David." Mr. Potter appeared on the scene in great good humour. "Was Elizabeth with you?"

Bugs nodded.

"Oh, I sure was, Mr. Potter," said Elizabeth enthusiastically. "I was helping him with his science project." She laughed. "It's just so fantastic! When you see it, you're going to burst with pride. Nobody but David here could have done anything quite like it. When he hands it in he'll get sixty easily."

Mr. Potter glowed. "Maybe you can give me a hint, Elizabeth. David's so secretive about it. What's the project about?"

"It's . . . " Elizabeth thought it over, then laughed delightedly. "It's about a lost tribe of Indians."

There was a shocked silence. For a moment one could have heard a pin drop on the beach at Lake Naka-mee-chee. Then every member of Elizabeth's admiring crowd took off on a dead run for his tent. In seconds Elizabeth, Bugs, Peter and Mr. Potter were the only people outside on the beach.

* * *

Scores of radio signals were being transmitted to museums all over the world, all emanating from the same point—Lake Naka-mee-chee. News of the lost tribe was met with great excitement and instant action in cities across the globe. Cashiers in museums everywhere were making long-distance phone calls to other museum cashiers. The news was spreading like wildfire.

Johnson switched off his transmitter and bit his lip with nervous tension. Soon some of his colleagues from the Museum of Anthropology would be here with videotape equipment. He prayed that they wouldn't be beaten by the Cicero team which would no doubt be arriving to help out Davis.

Davis prayed the same prayer in reverse. The Cicero had to be first. This was the discovery of the century!

In all the tents, urgent radio broadcasts were being made along with grim resolutions not to be second in line.

Benny put down his headphones and switched off the radio forlornly.

"What's going on?" asked Lesage. "Why didn't you report?" The news of a lost tribe had transcended even his love for Elizabeth.

"Uncle Vern's not there!" whined Benny. "I finally get a chance to call Uncle Vern, and he's not there!"

"Well, where is he?" demanded Lesage.

"They said he's going to be away for an extended period of time."

"But he can't be! We need him!"

"You should have let me call him earlier," Benny scolded. "Uncle Vern ought to be sore at *you!*"

"Uncle Vern ought to be sore? *We* ought to be sore at him for disappearing like this!"

Benny looked at him. "Oh—yeah."

Mikes from heaven

Lake Naka-mee-chee was big news. Word of the lost tribe had made its way to the front page of every major newspaper in the world. Excitement rose to a feverish pitch as the public awaited the momentous news that the twentieth century had finally "discovered" these primitives.

Radio and television crews, newspaper reporters and other press people were flocking up to Lake Naka-mee-chee along with scientists from every museum, cultural institution and university in the world.

Air Northland was completely booked. They had deployed all their seaplanes to the Naka-mee-chee run but still could not handle the demand. Other airlines were desperately searching maps to find Lake Naka-mee-chee and to establish regular flights there. Private helicopters and seaplane owners were demanding and getting outrageous prices to make the trip. Tent sales skyrocketed and all camping gear was at a premium. Canadian customs and immigration officers were working around the clock to process foreign applications for entry into the country.

When the lost Naka-mee-chee tribe entered the civilized world, the civilized world intended to be there to greet it.

* * *

Frank Potter was sleeping in. He turned over in his sleeping bag and stared at the ceiling of the tent.

He had been making an awful fool of himself, he reflected with some embarrassment. After all, what was the big fuss about a few people at Lake Naka-mee-chee? It certainly was unexpected, but they all had as much right to be there as he did. And if Regina wanted to organize social events, what harm did it do? She was entitled to enjoy herself, so if no one else minded, who was Frank Potter to complain? And David was right: he and John Vedda were pals. One camping trip shouldn't be allowed to spoil that.

He was going to get up and apologize like a man. Mary would be pleased. He'd apologize to John, Regina, Mary and even Gee for his surly behaviour. And then he'd do his best to make the rest of their trip a whole lot of fun.

He got up, dressed, put a benign smile on his face and stepped outside. An appalling sight met his eyes. The beach at Lake Naka-mee-chee was completely covered with tents—hundreds of them, staked out peg to peg. And they were all bustling with activity. There were people all over, carrying equipment and walking briskly in all directions.

He glanced at the waterfront. Four planes were letting people off. Planes and helicopters were circling, landing, coming and going, delivering more and more people. The air was filled with the roar of engines, the sound of voices and the hammering of tent pegs. How had he not noticed it before?

He took a sweeping panoramic look at his deserted wilderness paradise—wall-to-wall people. Then, without a word, he returned to his empty tent, zipped down the flap, got back into his pyjamas and went back to bed.

* * *

The Nickaninny was having a delicious breakfast of pancakes and syrup at a folding table behind Roger's cottage, overlooking his vegetable garden.

"You wouldn't believe it!" exclaimed Bugs. "Hundreds and hundreds of people! I mean, yesterday I was surprised to see thirty or forty, but today you can't even walk on the beach."

"Really?" said Roger with a worried frown. "I should probably report this to my superiors."

"Yeah," Gus laughed, "but that would mean . . . " He gestured with his knife and fork.

"That's not even the weird part," Bugs went on. "Some of those anthropologist guys wanted to interview *me*. Man, I got out of there in a hurry! Today my dad told them I went to the other side of the lake. That's where they all went this morning."

"Yesterday I said Bugs was doing his science project on a lost tribe of Indians," Elizabeth explained. "I think they all believed me. So much for the scientific community."

"Don't you think you'd better tell them the truth?" said Gus.

"Why?" smirked Elizabeth. "They're all great minds. It'll come to them."

"All I know is my dad is freaking out," said Bugs. "He came up here for solitude—that and to have me do my project."

Elizabeth laughed at the mere memory of Bugs' notes. "Why don't you do some of that now?" she suggested. "I really want to see how you guys generate that stuff."

"Nah," said Bugs. "I've done enough school this summer—nineteen pages. What more could my dad want? And we ran out of Nickaninnies to write about. Besides, who can think about boring stuff like that with our group going down?" His eyes sparkled as he recalled the previous day's session. "We are fantastic! I mean, we are terrific! I mean, we are the most! Even Elizabeth—I thought she'd stink, but she's great!"

"Thanks," said Elizabeth dryly. The thought of the group mellowed her enough that she let the left-handed compliment pass without comment.

"And our stuff!" Bugs raved on. "We do all the best groups' greatest songs. I almost can't believe it!" He sighed. "I honestly wonder if it's possible to be better off!"

* * *

A lone supply helicopter circled over Lake Naka-mee-chee. "It looks like Coney Island," said the pilot. "I've never seen such crowds in my life. You can hardly find the beach."

"Hmmm. Ramsay and Hyde can't be there," said his companion. "Sterling says their camp is isolated. Try somewhere in the woods."

They flew over the forest, keeping their eyes peeled for a possible campsite for their drop.

"There's something," said the pilot. "Looks like a little cottage. That has to be it."

"Okay," said the other man, "take her in for the drop."

The helicopter hovered in the air above the cottage. The second man checked the seal on the bulky foam-padded package, attached a parachute and dropped it out the helicopter door.

The pilot watched the falling equipment. "Chute opened perfectly, right on target. Let's go home."

The helicopter arced in the air and flew away.

* * *

The four members of The Nickaninny watched as an enormous parcel floated out of the blue and landed with a soft thud right in the centre of Roger's vegetable garden. The large parachute settled softly on and around it.

"My tomatoes!" exclaimed the ranger in dismay.

Roger was the first to reach the package. The others helped him move it out of the garden, but a large section of the tomato patch was already flattened.

"What can it be?" asked Gus.

"It's probably a tank," mourned Roger, looking at his crushed plants.

Bugs ripped the package open. He took out an expensive microphone and cradled it lovingly. "Mikes!" he cried in delight. "Mikes from heaven!"

The four gathered around the large box and examined the contents. Ramsay and Hyde's equipment consisted of several microphones, a sensitive reel-to-reel tape machine, two movie cameras, two still cameras and a variety of lighting equipment and film. There were also two large power packs.

"Tell you what The Nickaninny's going to do," announced Bugs decisively. "We're going to have a concert!"

"What?" chorused Gus, Roger and Elizabeth.

"A concert!" Bugs repeated, enthusiasm mounting. "When you've got a group, equipment and lots of people, you've got a concert. And that's exactly what we've got!"

"But what about your folks?" asked Gus.

"Oh, don't worry about them. When they see how great we are they won't be mad. They'll be proud!"

"My parents will be furious," put in Elizabeth. "They'll scream and rant and rave and—" A strange twinkle came into her eyes. "When's the concert?"

"No time like the present," said Bugs cheerily. "We'll do it tonight, around midnight."

"Are you sure about this?" asked Roger hesitantly.

"Of course I'm sure!"

"You know, Bugs," said Gus, "we all like The Nickaninny as much as you do, but a concert seems like"—he chose his words carefully—"well, a big step."

"That's what's so great about it! It's our biggest step. We have to be heard. We're amazing!"

"It's been a long time since I've seen my forestry manual," said Roger, "but I'm pretty sure I'm not supposed to sponsor—"

"There's only one problem," said Bugs thoughtfully. "We don't have an amp and speaker."

"Can't we use the speaker in your tape deck?" Elizabeth suggested.

Bugs shook his head. "It's not strong enough."

The group stood thinking, a little dejected. "Well," said Roger reluctantly, "we could always use the loudspeaker system in my helicopter."

"Helicopter?" echoed the others.

"Oh yes, didn't I mention it? All the rangers have patrol helicopters. I can't say I've ever used mine, but I keep it in good condition. Do you want to see it? The pad is just north of here."

Roger led the rest of the group to a cleared area beyond the garden. There sat a long green fibreglass bubble helicopter. On each side was mounted a large loudspeaker.

Bugs whistled in admiration. "Wow! How loud does it get?"

"Well," said Roger, "I haven't tried it out because I didn't want to create a disturbance, but the manual says it can be heard from the air across an enormous area. You see, it's supposed to be for warning campers of an emergency. But we never have emergencies. We never even had campers until this year."

"What are those big white things on the side?" asked Elizabeth.

"Water tanks. According to the manual they must be full at all times in case of forest fire. I never have fires, but I like to follow the rules." He added hopefully, "We won't be breaking any rules at the concert, will we?"

"This is fantastic!" raved Bugs ecstatically. "I've never been so happy in my life! This is going to be the best concert since The Glob filled Olympic Stadium and set off a volcano on stage!"

Elizabeth grinned. "How are we going to get people to come to our concert?"

"Don't worry," promised Bugs. "We'll figure it all out. Man, we are going to be mega-mega-mega-*amazing!*"

* * *

The hordes of anthropologists had returned from a fruitless search across the lake. Lesage, who hadn't slept all night, was worried. It would be entirely his fault if AMO were cut out of this discovery, all because he'd refused to radio Sterling in order to protect Elizabeth. Now Sterling was out of reach and *he* was alone with Benny—not the world's most capable assistant.

He looked out over the teeming beach to where Mrs. Vedda was scurrying from tent to tent, taking down names on a clipboard. Even at this point he couldn't decide what her purpose could possibly be. And his lovely Elizabeth was nowhere to be seen. He had lost her to—of all people—David Potter, who was probably really David Ramsay. But then again, she was likely Elizabeth Hyde. What a miserable muddle!

Lesage went over and sat beside his gloomy companion. "All right, Benny, our backs are up against the wall. It's up to the two of us to make sure AMO isn't left out of this."

"Left out of what?" asked Benny blankly.

"The discovery."

"What discovery?"

Lesage buried his face in his hands. "A lost tribe of Indians is about to be discovered up here somewhere. Ramsay and Hyde have known all about it from the beginning."

"Ramsay and Hyde?" queried Benny. "Where?"

Lesage pointed down the beach. "Right over there —the two men who call themselves Potter and Vedda."

"They aren't Ramsay and Hyde," said Benny. "I know Ramsay and Hyde. That's not them."

"It's *not?*" Lesage was horrified.

"No," said Benny, bewildered. "Why?" His face fell. "Oh, no! Don't tell me we infiltrated the wrong guys!"

Lesage nodded miserably.

"And don't tell me we kept radio silence all this time when we didn't have to! Boy, Uncle Vern's *really* going to be sore! I don't want to be around him when—"

"Benny!"

Dr. Vernon Sterling was marching up the crowded beach, threading his way among the tents.

Benny jumped to his feet and turned white. "It's Uncle Vern!" he whispered hoarsely. "And look how red he is! Man, is he sore!"

Lesage too got to his feet, his face still green from the shocking realization that he had been here a week and had not yet located Ramsay and Hyde.

"Benny, why didn't you call in?" bellowed Sterling.

"I did," said Benny in a small voice. "You weren't there."

"I mean before then!"

"We were keeping radio silence."

"Whose half-witted idea was that?" roared Sterling.

"His," said Benny.

Lesage smiled weakly.

"Why didn't you call in after you found Ramsay and Hyde?" Sterling demanded.

"I—I—I didn't find them, sir," stammered Lesage.

"You didn't find them?"

"Well, I thought I did, but it turned out not to be them."

Sterling turned to his nephew. "And you! A chimpanzee could be trained to follow such simple instructions. What did I do to deserve you? Why must I find out from the cafeteria cashier what two of my people could easily have told me but didn't because they were *stupid* enough to keep radio silence!"

"Excuse me, sir," came a voice, "but I take great exception to hearing you speak to Mr. Gee and Mr. Brent in this rough fashion."

Sterling whirled around and stared at Mrs. Vedda. "Who are *you?*"

"I am Regina Vedda, and I represent Mr. Gee and Mr. Brent."

"Who are *they?*"

"Why, the fine gentlemen you are yelling at. I don't know where you come from, sir, but at Lake Naka-mee-chee Mr. Gee and Mr. Brent are respected as pillars of the community."

Sterling wheeled to face Lesage and Benny.

"We're undercover," Benny whispered.

"It's okay, Mrs. Vedda," said Lesage. "He's our boss."

"Oh," she replied. "Uncle Vern who owns the welding shop. How do you do?" She scribbled his name onto her list. "I hope we can rely on you to join our Greater Lake Naka-mee-chee Tentowners' Association."

"Get her away from me!" muttered Sterling to Lesage.

"Uh—thank you very much, Mrs. Vedda. I'm sure Uncle Vern will join."

"Oh, that's splendid then." She walked on to another tent.

"Now," bawled Dr. Sterling, "I want to hear the whole story, right from the beginning!"

* * *

While several helicopters and planes circled the beach at Lake Naka-mee-chee waiting for room to land, a lone helicopter flew over an area completely out of view of the beach. Roger was at the controls, transporting the first load of equipment to the concert site. Bugs had dismissed anything in the area of the cave or Roger's house as too small for the expected turn-out. Instead he had chosen a sizable flat clearing with an elevated plateau-like area at one end, located about one kilometre from the beach.

Roger hovered over it now, and following Bugs' hand signals, set the craft down at the rear of the plateau, a sandstone table more than a metre higher than the rest of the clearing. It was to serve as The Nickaninny's stage. They began to unload the equipment, most of it from Ramsay and Hyde's shipment.

"I can't get over this spot!" Bugs exclaimed. "It's perfect for our concert! It's like they knew we were coming!"

Roger laughed nervously. "It *is* kind of tailor-made," he agreed, unloading his guitar and Gus's flute and placing them lovingly on the ground.

Bugs was establishing his drum set near the back, centre-stage. "Our audience is going to freak out!" he raved, eyes shining with anticipation. "Picture this: you're bored because you're stuck at Lake Nickaninny. Suddenly there's this fantastic rock concert! Wow!"

The ranger smiled weakly. "I guess we have the element of surprise on our side."

"And the best group ever to come out of the Nickaninny woods!" Bugs added. "Okay, I'll wait here. You go back for the next load."

Gus and Elizabeth sat on Roger's front doorstep behind an enormous pile of lamps and lighting fixtures.

"This is crazy!" said Elizabeth with a wide grin. "Only Bugs Potter could start something like this. I'm dying to see what he's going to do with all these lamps."

Gus was preoccupied and unhappy looking. "Mmmm," he said.

"I just can't wait until the concert tonight!" Elizabeth rattled on. "If Bugs runs a concert the way he writes a science project, it *will* be the biggest thing since The Glob set off a volcano on stage. Come on, Gus, brighten up. You should be laughing. What's eating you?"

"My heritage."

"What heritage?"

"That's just it," said Gus. "I've met three nice people and I'm having a great time, but my father sent me up here to find my heritage—I'm not even *looking* for it. Instead of playing ritual music to the spirits I'm playing Spoon Rest. I should be building the things my ancestors built, not helping set up a stage. And I should be living off the land, not eating out of a ranger's freezer. Face it. I stink at being an Indian!"

"Come off it," Elizabeth scoffed. "If you've lived in New York all your life, there's no way your father expects you to go back two hundred years and live like an Indian."

Gus looked up bleakly. "Yes he does. He said so."

"I'll bet he didn't say that. I'll bet that's just what you heard. Your father sent you up here to see what it's like, maybe to make an effort to live life the old way, and to *feel* your heritage."

Gus looked at her oddly. "My father used that word too—feel. But I thought he was just being a cornball."

"You've felt it," said Elizabeth, "and made more than an effort, so now you can take Roger's painting of you as an Indian and go home proud of a job well done."

Gus smiled and nodded. "Elizabeth, you're terrific!" He slapped his forehead suddenly. "Oh, no! That means I've been busting my butt making arrows and spears and war masks, getting splinters and cuts and bruises, all for nothing. And all those nuts and berries—the cramps I've had! And I didn't really have to do it. I could kill myself!"

Elizabeth giggled. "That was part of the effort."

Gus slumped back and indulged in a laugh at himself. "Well, here comes Roger with the helicopter. We'd better get this stuff over to the pad."

* * *

Ramsay and Hyde were perched in their tree above the teaming megalopolis that was the beach.

"Why me?" mourned Ramsay. "All I wanted to do was revolutionize the world of anthropology. Was that asking too much?"

"How did all these people get here?" asked Hyde.

"News of my—I mean *our*—lost tribe must have leaked somehow. Planes have been coming in by the dozens every day—everyone's breaking his neck to get here. Tonight's the eclipse and we have no equipment. So much for Sterling! When I see him I'll tell him a thing or two!"

"Go ahead," said Hyde. "If I'm not mistaken, that's him down there with Lesage and Benny."

Ramsay squinted. "You're right! It's Sterling—he must have brought our equipment personally! We must speak to him at once!"

The two shinnied down the tree and began threading their way across the crowded beach to where Sterling sat with his nephew and Lesage.

"You have made such a hash of this," Dr. Sterling was saying to Lesage, "that you've likely cost AMO a discovery right in our own back yard. And what I'd like to do to you is nothing compared with what I'd like to do to Ramsay and Hyde! All this is really their fault!"

"Well, you could do it to them right now, Uncle Vern," said Benny. "Here they come."

Sterling leapt to his feet. "Ramsay! Hyde! What's the meaning of this?"

"I haven't got time to explain it now," said Ramsay briskly. "Where's our equipment?"

"The equipment? *You* have it! It went out early this morning!"

"But we never received anything," said Hyde.

Ramsay was horrified. "You mean, at the crucial moment your museum has lost our equipment? Or worse still, given it to somebody else?"

"None of this would have happened if you hadn't been so secretive!" cried Sterling.

"All right, all right," said Ramsay. "We must remain calm. We still have an advantage over this horde of people." He threw his arms out in despair. "But even if we get there first we still don't have any equipment to record the event!"

"I've got the Polaroid camera Uncle Vern gave me for my sixteenth birthday," piped up Benny.

"We can use that to prove we were there," said Sterling.

"Maybe," said Ramsay. He looked nervously at the people milling around the beach. "We'd better discuss this in private."

One by one Ramsay, Hyde, Sterling, Lesage and Benny filed into Lesage's tent.

* * *

"Everything's ready," said Bugs, setting the microphones in place in front of his drum set.

Gus experimentally brought his flute up to the microphone stand in front of him.

"Don't play anything," said Bugs quickly. "The system's not on anyway, but we wouldn't want to give away our surprise."

Roger brought his thumb down a centimetre away from the strings of his guitar in a mock strum. The weight of the guitar seemed slightly awkward now that there was a pick-up microphone taped inside. "Okay. Complete silence."

Elizabeth giggled in anticipation. "I can't wait! It's going to be—it's going to be indescribable!"

"Well, don't get nervous, Elizabeth," Bugs cautioned.

She laughed in his face. "I wouldn't worry."

Roger looked at his watch. "Well, we've got six hours before the concert. How are we going to kill the time?"

"Supper," said Bugs. "Elizabeth and I have to go back so our folks won't get suspicious. But one of you guys better stay here on guard. After supper I'll sneak out of camp, we'll do the last-minute setting up and run through the songs in our minds so no one forgets the order. Then we lure all the people and the concert starts."

"How are we going to do that?" asked Gus. "Get the people here, I mean?"

"I've got it all worked out," said Bugs, eyes dancing. "Okay, now listen . . . "

Live via satellite

At eleven o'clock that night the five-man contingent from AMO crept out of Lesage's tent in single file, Sterling in the lead, Lesage and Benny following, and Ramsay and Hyde bringing up the rear. They snaked their way through the jigsaw of tents, careful to make their footsteps as quiet as possible on the sand and pebbles. The beach, though packed with people, seemed fairly quiet. Almost everyone had retired early in confusion and frustration when the lost tribe of Indians failed to materialize. Most of them had come to the conclusion that Mr. Potter had lied about his son to put them off the track; and they intended to scour the woods behind the beach the next day.

Moving very carefully, the AMO party continued purposefully towards the shelter of the trees. Their pace increased slightly as they moved through the last alleyway between the last two rows of tents and felt the cool of the forest.

Just as Sterling reached the woods, he suddenly jolted forward and fell flat on his face with a loud cry.

"Aha!" Johnson came running out of the under-brush, followed by several of his colleagues from the New York Museum of Anthropology. "Didn't I tell you Davis and his bunch would try to sneak out on us? Well, our trip-wire sure stopped them! It—" Suddenly Johnson was in the air, landing with a thud in some bushes. "Hey, who put a trip-wire over here?"

Davis leapt out of the shadows. "Aha! The Cicero triumphs once again!" He and his staff began running toward the bushes where Johnson had fallen, but all six of them hit the first trip-wire and landed sprawled around Sterling.

"Uncle Vern!" yelled Benny. "Are you all right?"

"Davis!" bellowed Johnson, standing up and picking burrs out of his clothes.

"Johnson, I'll get you!" Davis grabbed Sterling by the shoulders and glared into his face. "You're not Johnson!"

"Of course not!" said Sterling, getting to his feet. "May I ask what lunatic strung wires here?"

"Him!" chorused Johnson and Davis, pointing at each other, but their attention was diverted when they heard voices coming from the beach.

"Hey, what's going on over there?"

There was the sound of running feet, and then three Washington anthropologists bounded into the woods and tumbled over the trip-wire.

"Let's get away from the trees," said Sterling with authority, "before someone gets killed."

"Someone's going to get killed!" promised Johnson. "If I knew where that trip-wire was, I'd stroll right around it and a certain someone would get his face punched in!"

"Someone from the Museum of Anthropology!" came Davis's voice.

There were more running feet and bobbing flashlights appeared all over the beach.

"Now look what you've done!" accused Johnson. "You woke everybody up!"

Ramsay, who was trying to sneak off into the woods, was grabbed bodily by the Head of Anthropology at Ethan Allen University, who sometimes worked out with the football team.

"Just where did you think you were going?"

"Unhand me, sir!"

Another group of new arrivals rushed onto the scene and scattered as they hit the trip-wires.

The voice of one of the men on the ground split the air. "Nobody's going to leave this beach and make any discoveries without *me!*"

"All right!" Ramsay bellowed. "Everybody march one by one—careful of the wires—back to the beach where we can all see each other and discuss this like gentlemen."

Slowly and with much muttering, the anthropologists began to make their way out of the woods. Satisfied to see the process in motion, Ramsay turned around and headed in the other direction. He felt an iron grip on his shoulder.

"We tolerate no welchers at AMO," came Sterling's cold voice.

By now the beach was alive with flashlights and lanterns. People were rushing about in every direction and shouting, some in foreign languages, but all with only one purpose in mind. No matter what it was that was going on, no one intended to be left out, thereby bringing disgrace to his respective museum, university, institution, television network, radio station, newspaper or magazine.

Mrs. Vedda elbowed her way right into the centre of the loudest shouting. "What on earth is going on here? Gentlemen, gentlemen, *please!*"

The shouting died down gradually until the beach was almost completely silent. This was it—the moment of truth. Surely now this Mrs. Vedda would abandon the pretense of the Tentowners' Association and reveal her true purpose.

"Well, that's much better," said Mrs. Vedda. "I must say that I'm extremely disappointed in the behaviour of some of our members."

The crowd waited expectantly.

"If we are going to have a Greater Lake Naka-mee-chee Tentowners' Association, our members will simply have to learn to conduct themselves in a manner that is suitable to a social organization of this nature."

By now everyone was awake and hundreds of eyes and ears were focused on Mrs. Vedda.

"So why don't we all go back to sleep and forget that this dreadful incident ever took place?"

An uneasy murmur spread like a ripple. She hadn't said anything about the lost tribe!

Hyde stood in the middle of the restless mob, confused and disappointed. All their work had turned into this mess, a snarl so complex that it would take a team of trouble-shooters months to figure out what was really going on. Then suddenly he was staring towards the far end of the beach. Just inside the woods a torch burned brightly.

"Hey!" he cried, pointing at it.

For a second everyone stared, transfixed. Then pandemonium swept the scene. There was a stampede back to the tents for notepads, TV cameras and tape recorders, and then a rush towards the torch. The entire population of the teeming beach swarmed at the edge of the trees around the brightly-burning beacon.

"Hey, look!"

There, about twenty metres deeper into the woods, was another flaming torch.

"Where are we going?" Frank Potter asked his wife. "Where's David?"

"He's gone again," she replied, "and something awfully strange is happening."

The mass of people and equipment surged on through the dense woods as yet a third torch became visible.

* * *

The small television screen showed a lavish ballroom filled with Victorian ladies and gentlemen. "Thank you for the dance," said the hero, a naval officer. "May I procure you some refreshment—a glass of lemonade perhaps?"

Suddenly the screen went blue and the words *Special Report* flashed across it. A voice said: "We interrupt this program to bring you a special report live via satellite from Lake Naka-mee-chee, Ontario. Here is special correspondent Richard Mann."

"Oh my!" said the lady sitting on the couch next to her husband. "It's that Lake Naka-mee-chee— you know, from the paper this morning. They must have found that lost tribe of Indians. Isn't this exciting?"

Her husband grunted. "Whatever it is, it's got to be better than that lousy movie."

The screen showed the pitch-black forest of Lake Naka-mee-chee, and in the foreground, one of the torches.

"This is Richard Mann reporting from Lake Naka-mee-chee. The greatest anthropological minds in the world have converged on this remote wilderness area to be greeted by this scene—one flaming torch in a long line of similar torches. What can it mean? Scientists believe that at the end of this trail they will find the lost tribe of Naka-mee-chee, a clan of Indians that time all but forgot until this momentous night."

The camera panned to a shot of Richard Mann with a surging crowd of people following the line of torches. "Excuse me, sir," said the newsman to one of the crowd. "What's your name?"

"Dr. Ramsay."

"Would you like to tell us, Dr. Ramsay, your interpretation of what's going on here?"

"No, I would not. Mind your own business!"

"Uh—you, sir. What's *your* name?"

"Johnson."

"What can you tell us about what's happening tonight?"

"I would just like to say for the record that the New York Museum of Anthropology is right here on the spot, ready for whatever might happen."

Another head came into view. "And the Cicero Institute was here first!"

Richard Mann moved hastily away. "Ah, sir, please introduce yourself."

"Oh, hi. I'm Benny."

"Tell us, Benny—what's your impression of this situation?"

"Oh, it's real creepy! I mean, with the torches and all that. Creepiest thing I've ever seen. Really gives me the creeps!"

"Uh—yes. Thank you. Oh, ma'am. Hello, ma'am. You seem rather upset—"

"Of course I'm upset! My Tentowners' Association is falling to pieces! Wouldn't you be upset?"

A man walked by the camera and muttered, "Some vacation!"

Richard Mann looked hopelessly into the camera for a moment, then said, "Well, as you can see, excitement is running high in the scientific community, and the tension is certainly getting to people." There was a wide shot of the crowd. "We've been walking for over ten minutes now and—yes! We seem to have come to some kind of clearing! For those of you who have just tuned in, we've come to a large clearing! It's very dark. All we can really see is the torch. It seems to be—yes it is! The last torch! Now all the crowd is filing into the clearing here. It's absolutely pitch dark. The only light is the dim glow from the torch, some flashlights and the lighting crews' equipment. There's hardly any moonlight. Wait a minute—I've just been informed that right now we are experiencing an eclipse of the moon! This is incredible! You can feel the excitement in the air! Any second now we will be face to face with the past—the lost tribe of Naka-mee-chee!"

The lady on the sofa leaned forward. "Oooh, isn't it exciting?"

Her husband snored.

* * *

Clutching their equipment, the scientists and reporters stood shoulder to shoulder in the blackness of the clearing. The broadcasters were everywhere, ready to relate whatever story was about to break. The crowd was a unit now, surging and quivering like a giant amoeba. A hush fell as people began to wonder what would happen next.

Dr. Hyde stared up at the sky. The last sliver of moon slipped into eclipse.

BOOM! The sound split the air, its sheer volume shaking the crowd and knocking some people backwards.

BOOM! The ground shook. Then there was a blinding flash of white light so intense that the spectators had to shield their eyes.

There was another tremendous boom, and another, until the sound became a steady pounding, the bright light pulsating to the rhythm, casting flashing shadows over the shocked crowd. A new sound began to swell—a low, distorted strummed note, vibrating in beat with the pounding. The sound grew faster and louder. People clamped their hands over their ears and tried to squint around the blinding flashes to see what was really behind them. The pulsing sounds grew to an ear-splitting level, joined by a high-pitched wailing noise that climbed ever higher with the beat. The sound reached a murderous crescendo, followed by a colossal crash and a ring of lights blinked on, revealing on their sandstone stage The Nickaninny.

Positively glowing with excitement and purpose, Bugs Potter threw himself at the drums. Bouncing up and down on his seat, his drumsticks a blur, he beat like a madman, the amplified sounds from his crude drum set blasting out at the crowd. He assaulted his audience with volume, hammering out machine-gun rhythms and calling upon all his skill. He was dazzlingly brilliant, opening with a solo, as Gus and Roger stood staring at him, shocked into inactivity by the excitement he was generating.

Recovering themselves, they crashed in, playing furiously along with Bugs. Roger strummed madly at his guitar and Gus brought his flute right up to the microphone. The speakers at either end of the stage roared at the shocked spectators, who stood like statues, staring in bewilderment.

At the rear of the stage stood Roger's helicopter, lights blinking and blades slowly rotating. The door opened and out jumped Elizabeth Vedda, clutching her microphone. She let out a piercing shriek and then began to strut arrogantly to the front of the stage.

The crowd came to life with a hoarse cry of recognition. Elizabeth stood before them wearing Roger's large Department of Forestry shirt, which hung down far enough to cover completely her cut-off shorts. Her hair was rolled up under a ranger's hat, and on her feet she wore Gus's native moccasins. Around her neck hung a heavy pair of binoculars. She screamed one more time and then began singing the big Endomorph hit, "Blast It," accompanied in fine style by the rest of The Nickaninny. She strutted smartly before them, executing cartwheels and ballet movements and occasionally crouching down to peer at the crowd through her binoculars.

A roar of laughter and cheering was beginning to swell from the audience, especially from the ranks of those who had studied Elizabeth so carefully the same way.

Mr. Vedda was at the rear of the clearing, standing on tiptoe and shaking his fist. "Elizabeth! You come away from there *this minute!*" No one heard him over the roar of the music.

Frank Potter stared in amazement at his son and the drums. It was unbelievable. He had taken David up to the back of beyond to get him away from his stereo, and the boy had managed to form a rock group!

Dr. Ramsay gawked at the stage in disbelief. "There must be some mistake..."

Benny tapped his uncle on the shoulder. "Uncle Vern, uh—I don't think this is the lost tribe of Naka-mee-chee."

Vernon Sterling was white with rage. Imagine! The time wasted, the expense, the disgrace of being associated with such an event!

"Keep shooting! Keep shooting!" cried Richard Mann to his camera crew.

"But boss, we're on the air live! And these ain't no Indians!"

"Shoot anyway! This could be big!"

All over the clearing cameras and tape recorders rolled and commentators babbled excitedly.

On stage the group crashed to a tremendous finish. Bugs hit the main switch and all the lights went out. A chorus of laughing cheers came from the audience. Then Bugs turned on the main searchlight and trained it on Elizabeth's back, casting her shadow across the clearing.

"Hello, everybody!" Elizabeth screamed. "How are you tonight?"

The response was a wave of laughter.

"We're The Nickaninny, and we'd like to welcome you all to our opening night here at Lake Naka-mee-chee. And a special greeting to all you anthropologists out there!"

A big cheer went up.

"And to all you welders!"

"Hooray!" cried Benny, who wasn't sure whether or not he was still under cover.

"All *right!*" Elizabeth went on, assuming a Bugs Potter vocabulary. "There's electricity in the air and we're all into rock, so let's get moving with this little number by Toast—it's called 'Burn My Bread'!"

The lights came back on and Bugs, Gus and Roger broke into the number. Elizabeth sang, running around, jumping and performing gymnastic manoeuvres:

You can pull my hair, you can step on my face,
You can gouge my eyes—any time, any place,
You can kick in my knees and bash in my head,
But whatever you do, don't burn my bread!

The group embarked on an instrumental while Elizabeth ran up and down the stage staring out at her audience through the binoculars. From what she could see, the reaction was mixed. Some people were laughing their heads off, some were livid with rage and others looked completely lost. She saw a television camera and was taken aback for an instant. What was a TV station doing here? No, two stations —three—more! The whole audience was dotted with TV and newsreel cameras! CTV! CBS! *BBC?* The world was watching! She let the binoculars hang and ran back across the stage to the drum set.

"Bugs! You'd better know—"

"Not now, Elizabeth!" he cried, in the middle of a spectacular solo. "We're a smash!"

Elizabeth tried to say something again, then shrugged and resumed her position at the front of the stage. Oh well, if all this was funny for hundreds of people, it might just be funny for millions of them. She cringed at the thought of the millions, then gave a great shriek as the band crashed to a finish.

"All right, everybody! I'm sure a number of you have heard of this next song. It's called 'Swan Lake.' Most of you know it the way Tchaikovsky wrote it— this is the version by Flaming Sidewalks. All right, let's go!"

Bugs beat out a drum roll and the band roared into the rock adaptation:

Take me to the lake where the swans hang out!
That's where it's at!
Swan Lake! Oh, yeah! . . .

Howls of laughter rang through the clearing. When the song finished The Nickaninny swung right into "Dirty Socks" by The Feet.

"Well, folks, Richard Mann here, still at Lake Naka-mee-chee, where a most unexpected thing has happened—we're still not quite sure what. It looks as if the lost tribe of Naka-mee-chee is really some sort of elaborate hoax to publicize this rock group called The Nickaninny, obviously a corruption of the word Naka-mee-chee."

Davis jumped in front of the camera. "And I would like to say that the Cicero Institute knew it all along!"

"Elizabeth!" howled Mr. Vedda. "Stop this!"

Mrs. Vedda was staring in disbelief. How could all this be happening without consultation with the Tentowners' Association?

"Do you see our son?" Mrs. Potter shouted over the din.

Her husband was seated on the ground, still staring bug-eyed at the spectacle of his son on the stage. He made no reply.

Lesage stared dumbly at Elizabeth. This was certainly a side of her he'd never seen before.

"Isn't this great, Uncle Vern?" cried Benny, snapping his fingers to the heavy beat. "That guy is some drummer!"

Dr. Sterling looked at him with loathing. "Just don't talk to me."

The number ended with Elizabeth throwing herself up in the air and landing in a split with her binoculars focused out on the crowd. There was a tremendous roar from the audience. Most of the anthropologists were now taking the concert for what it was and using it as an outlet for relief from the enormous tension and competition over who would be the first to find the lost tribe.

"Now we'd like to feature one of the most—different—people in the world! On drums, our founder and driving force, *Bugs Potter!* Here is a song by The Glob called 'Godzilla Meets the Little Drummer Boy.'"

Very quietly Bugs began a regular military drumming and Gus played the drummer boy theme on his flute. Suddenly Elizabeth let out a savage bestial roar and Bugs exploded into a wild, breathtaking performance that had many members of the audience actually cheering. Bugs Potter and The Nickaninny were beginning to come across as musicians as well as the biggest joke in anthropological history.

"As you can see and hear," Richard Mann was raving, "The Nickaninny is no amateur group. Just the fact that their equipment looks as though it was thrown together in a few minutes shows the true professionalism that was used to fool the entire scientific community of the world. Yes, folks, it's all a hoax—but *what* a hoax!"

Bugs was still drumming up complete pandemonium, accompanied by Gus and Roger with Elizabeth screaming out the part of Godzilla. Now the audience was roaring with laughter and approval.

"Why is everybody laughing?" Ramsay screamed at Hyde.

Hyde shrugged miserably.

A young reporter from an Australian newspaper slapped them both on the back. "Come on, you two crabs, relax. It's a great show!"

Ramsay cast him a withering glare. "Just who are you?"

"Nevin. Science editor of my paper. But I double

as the rock critic." He patted his notebook. "Good thing, too."

Johnson pushed all his staff in front of Richard Mann's TV cameras. "Okay, guys, laugh!" As the crew began to chuckle and guffaw Johnson announced, "This is just to show you what good sports we are at the Museum of Anthropology in New York. We admit it—we were fooled. But you don't see us trying any fancy cover-ups like the Cicero."

The song ended with a long drum roll and a stunning victory for Godzilla. The band swung right into selections from *Hay, Man,* a classic album by Thoroughbred.

Frank Potter was now leaning against a tree for support, but his eyes never left the stage. There were the missing pots. Of course. He had never thought for a minute that David would be using them for drums, but David had not only made drums, he had created two other musicians from thin air. His father should have known when the complaints about Lake Naka-mee-chee stopped, when David was no longer asking to go home, that something was afoot. He should have known that David could never be satisfied with anything that wasn't rock music. He should have known!

Peter Vedda tugged at Dr. Sterling's jacket. "Hey, mister," he said proudly, "see the lead singer there? That's *my* sister! What do you think of that?"

Sterling, who was still seeing red, made no reply.

The cameras rolled on. "This is Richard Mann, your Lake Naka-mee-chee correspondent, still here live. The show goes on, and what a show it is! The Nickaninny is adding just the right mixture of hard

rock, humour and showmanship to their performance, and this crowd of disappointed scientists is
loving it. It's been going on for almost an hour and
the moon has reappeared from the earth's shadow.
Everyone's question here is: 'How long will this momentous concert continue?'"

Elizabeth supplied the anwer. "Okay, everybody,
this is our last set. Songs by Endomorph, The Glob,
Iced Tea, Volcanohead and Flabber-Gas. All right,
here we go!"

The Nickaninny exploded into Endomorph's version of "The Three Little Pigs" in which the two
pigs whose houses had been blown down by the wolf
moved to Florida on the insurance money and the
pig in the brick house was assessed for street repairs.
The clearing rocked with the heavy beat and the
crowd stamped their feet and clapped to the music.
It brought out the best in the musicians, who played
as they had never played before. Sweat was flying in
all directions as Bugs laboured over the drums. Roger's hands were red and sore as he strummed and
chorded furiously. Gus's mouth and cheeks ached,
and Elizabeth's long-trained operatic voice was a
hoarse rasp. She was screaming the part in which
the wolf identifies himself as the tax man and takes
off his wolf suit when Roger suddenly stopped playing and stared at the back of the clearing.

One of the torches had been knocked over and
some brush was burning.

"*Fire!*" he cried, throwing his guitar to the
ground. The microphone inside the instrument
jarred loose and bounced. A tremendous knocking
noise blasted out of the speakers, followed by a

painful squeal of feedback. With a few sparks and a wisp of smoke out of each speaker, The Nickaninny's sound system was dead.

"The amps!" cried Bugs in agony.

"Fire!" shouted Roger again. He leapt across the stage, threw himself into the helicopter and revved the already operating engine. The blades began to spin, creating a wind that blew most of The Nickaninny's lights over. Elizabeth's hat flew from her head and sailed over the crowd.

"It's a fire—a forest fire!" bellowed Richard Mann to his TV audience. "Could this be part of the act? Is it another hoax?"

Roger and the helicopter lifted up into the air. The speakers and searchlight, detached but still wired to the craft, dangled above the crowd. All eyes were on the helicopter, which had moved to a hover position over the fire.

In his first official act as forest ranger of Lake Naka-mee-chee, Roger Forrest opened up both water tanks. There was a roar as rivers of water fell from the sky, quenching the fire and soaking the people nearby. The spray drenched the clearing, short-circuiting TV cameras, tape recorders and even the stage lights as water splashed in all directions. Hardest hit were the members of the audience nearest the back, but everyone, including Bugs, Gus and Elizabeth on stage, was sprayed from head to toe.

Television sets all over the world went blank.

"What a finalé for The Nickaninny!" howled Richard Mann.

"Forget it, boss," said his cameraman. "We're shorted out."

"Aw, nuts!"

Roger flew back to the stage and landed the helicopter. The rush of water had smashed searchlight and speakers. He would have to report this. Boy, was he ever in trouble!

From behind the drums Bugs looked around at the wreckage. All that had been solid ground was now mud, and many members of the audience lay strewn about, dripping with water and muck.

Frank Potter stood in the middle of the shocked, soaking crowd, wringing water out of his shirt. A look of bewilderment still on his face, he felt a blow on his shoulder and wheeled to face a mountain of mud.

"John?"

The mountain scowled menacingly, causing small droplets of mud and grass to fall from him. "Potter, this is all your fault, you and that miserable son of yours! Luring my family up here on the pretense of a vacation and coercing my innocent young daughter to make a spectacle of herself on the stage! I'll kill you! No, that's too good for you—I'll sue! No, even better, I'll lay criminal charges against you and that hoodlum you call a son! I'll get the best lawyer in the country and he'll—"

"My son," interrupted Frank Potter, tight-lipped, "is *not* a hoodlum. He is the very *best* drummer in the world! And don't you *ever* forget it!"

Bugs stepped to the centre of the stage beside a sopping Elizabeth and Gus. He cupped his hands to his mouth. "Uh—the show's over, everybody! We hope you liked it! Thank you on behalf of the group!"

There was a shocked silence, then someone laughed.

"Lady," came a well-known voice from the muddiest part of the clearing, "next time you have a rock concert, issue life jackets!"

By the light of the moon the entire audience dissolved into howls of raucous laughter.

Back to civilization

Morning came bright and sunny at Lake Naka-mee-chee. The radio and television people had spent the remainder of the night repairing and drying out their equipment, and now the entire population was assembled on the beach attending a large press conference in honour of The Nickaninny.

Bugs, Gus, Roger and Elizabeth sat side by side at camp tables, fielding questions from the press.

"Well, we got the idea for The Nickaninny," Bugs was saying, "because things were so boring here that a guy could die. Gus, Roger and I played together, and we were so great we decided to form a rock group. Then Elizabeth joined, and there we were."

"And the equipment was all yours?"

"Well, we made the drums," Bugs explained, "and Gus had a flute and Roger had his own guitar. The speakers came with Roger's helicopter, and the rest of the stuff—the mikes, some lights and a bunch of cameras—just dropped out of the sky into Roger's tomato patch yesterday while we were having breakfast."

Ramsay glared at Sterling.

Someone put up his hand. "Excuse me, do you mean to say that you weren't planning to have a rock concert when you came up here?"

"Of course not," said Bugs. "Elizabeth and I got dragged up here by our parents for a camping trip. We didn't even know about Gus and Roger then."

One reporter shook his head. "It's a fantastic success story. Tell me, where does The Nickaninny go from here?"

"Back to civilization," announced Elizabeth, "never again to return to Lake Naka-mee-chee."

"Back to New York," said Gus. "That's where I live."

"I'm going to go home and drum!" said Bugs enthusiastically. "Pots and jeans and things are okay in a pinch, but the real thing—wow! And of course," he added, subdued, "I've got to hand in my make-up science project."

"I've been fired," said Roger mournfully. "Every week for two-and-a-half years I've called in and said that all was quiet. And this week they found out that it wasn't, so they fired me."

"What are you going to do?" asked a reporter.

"Well, I was thinking of trying my hand at art. I've done a little painting while I was here."

"Roger's coming home with me for a while," Gus added. "He can talk with my father about Lake Naka-mee-chee."

"Why don't you stay together as a group?" asked a radio newsman. "You could probably be very successful."

"Yeah, well," said Bugs, "my dad would never go

for it. He has old-fashioned ideas about high school and stuff."

"Besides," said Roger, "it would mean..." He gestured helplessly.

"Why doesn't one of you make a closing statement?" suggested Richard Mann, whose cameras were recording the conference.

"Okay," said Bugs. "On behalf of the group I'd like to thank everyone for coming and making our concert a success. And I'd like to say that I sure hope I pass with my science project."

* * *

In the afternoon, float planes and helicopters started arriving to ferry people home, and the population of Lake Naka-mee-chee began to dwindle.

Mrs. Vedda was fully occupied with saying farewell to everyone and taking a snapshot of each for her personal collection, chatting about some of the good times of the Tentowners' Association. She wrote down the address of each person, promising faithfully to send him a copy of the newsletter she was planning to publish.

It was the anthropologist from Boston who could restrain himself no longer. Before he boarded the plane he looked Mrs. Vedda straight in the eye. "All right, lady, it's all over. You've won, so let's have it. I admit complete defeat and so does everyone else. Tell me—*please* tell me—what were you really up to?"

She dimpled. "I was just trying to see that everyone had a wonderful time."

He eyed her suspiciously. "You're The Nickaninny's manager, right?"

179

"Oh, goodness, no," she said. "Well, goodbye. I'll send you our first newsletter as soon as it's ready."

"Okay. 'Bye, lady," he muttered, boarding the plane. Maybe she'd explain it in the newsletter.

* * *

Bugs, Gus and Roger walked along the shore, well satisfied with themselves.

"So it's settled," said Bugs. "I can stay at your house when I go to New York for the big Dorchester Melon concert August twenty-ninth."

Gus nodded. "Yes, but you've got to promise to practise. It's Naka-mee-chee, not Nickaninny. *Naka-mee-chee.* If you call my dad Mr. Nickaninny we're both in a lot of trouble."

"Don't worry. I'll have it perfect by then." He patted his notebook, which was jammed into his back pocket. "Well, tomorrow I go home. Hmmm. I'll have to pick a good time to show my dad my science project—you know, when he's in a mellow mood."

"I'd be very careful about that if I were you," said Gus. "Make sure he's *really* mellow. But don't feel bad—I'm in the same boat. My father probably saw me on TV, and I understand The Nickaninny's making the cover of *Time* this week."

"He'll be real proud of you," Bugs assured him. "After all, look at all the publicity we got for the Nickaninny Indians. And he's the chief."

"Just the same, first thing tomorrow morning I'll start work on some explanations and excuses."

They were walking by the AMO campsite when the strident voice of Dr. Sterling reached them. The chief anthropologist was lecturing Ramsay and Hyde.

"If you two had put on clown suits you couldn't have made bigger idiots of yourselves. Not only have you wasted the time of every respected anthropologist in the world, but you wasted an AMO grant chasing after nothing for three months. Not to mention how many years of personal research effort. There is no lost tribe of Naka-mee-chee!"

Bugs ran up to them, followed by Gus and Roger. "Excuse me, sir, but that's not right. There *is* a lost tribe."

"What?"

"Look at Gus here. He's a full-blooded Nickaninny Indian."

"He means Naka-mee-chee Indian," Roger corrected.

"Is this true?" stammered Ramsay, eyes wide.

"Sure," said Bugs. "The only reason you can't find them is because they all moved away." He pulled out his notebook. "In here I have all the information on all the Nickaninnies—you know, where they're living, who they married, who their kids are, what they do for a living ... "

Sterling began to read through the notebook, then looked up in confusion.

"You get used to the writing style after a while," said Gus.

"This is astonishing!" said Sterling. "Would we be able to interview your family? Would your father consent to talk about his ancestry?"

"Are you kidding?" said Gus. "He never shuts up about his ancestry. He always complains that our tribe never gets any recognition. He'll be thrilled!"

"Why, it's a first for AMO!" cried Sterling.

"I was right!" crowed Ramsay.

"*We* were right," Hyde amended.

"On behalf of the Anthropological Museum of Ontario," said Sterling, "I wish to purchase these notes. What's the price?"

"It's not for sale," said Bugs. "It's my make-up science project. If I don't hand it in I flunk, and then my dad'll kill me."

"You can't fail science, young man!" exclaimed Sterling. "Not after discovering and chronicling a lost Indian tribe!"

Bugs looked faintly pleased.

"Don't worry," said Gus. "All you need is my father. He'll tell you everything you need to know. I'll give you his address, and I can assure you that by the time he's finished telling you about our ancestry and our tribal customs, you'll be good and sick of us Naka-mee-chees."

"I don't think so, young man," said Ramsay, flushed with triumph. "I don't think so."

* * *

The population of Lake Naka-mee-chee continued to dwindle. The media people left, loaded with stories and interviews, and the anthropologists began to file home too, empty-handed and a little embarrassed.

Johnson and Davis left almost simultaneously. They parted still battling over who, out of sheer intelligence and ingenuity, had stayed drier during the previous night's water bombing.

The AMO party left in great good humour. Ramsay and Hyde were happy because they had been right all along and fame and fortune were just around the corner. Sterling was pleased with his first for AMO. Benny was relieved that Uncle Vern didn't seem to be sore anymore. And Lesage was overjoyed because he had received grudging permission to call Elizabeth the next time he was in Winnipeg.

The next morning the Potters and Veddas awoke to find the Porta-Toilet, gleaming in the early sun, sitting on the sand outside their tents, casting a long shadow down the beach. Attached to it was a short note of apology, unsigned.

The plane came for them an hour later. Before boarding, Mr. Potter and Mr. Vedda scanned the deserted beach and clasped hands in renewed friendship.

"Well, John," smiled Mr. Potter, "it didn't turn out the way we planned it, but at least we're friends again."

"Right, Frank. And we're this much smarter. Just wait till we hit the girls with next year's vacation plans!"

"Don't you dare!" said Mrs. Potter warningly.

"But honestly, Mary," said her husband, "it'll really be different next time!"

"Tell me about it later, Frank. Or better still don't tell me about it at all."

They boarded the plane, and as it took off, Bugs looked back at the beach.

Gus and Roger were standing there waving and pointing at something they had scrawled in the sand. As the plane gained altitude Bugs was able to make out the large letters:

AUG 29

NY

He reached forward and tapped his father on the shoulder. "Hey, Dad, could you ask the guy to fly this plane a little faster? I'm dying to get home and listen to some music!"